THE HOLIDAY HUSSY

MERRY FARMER

THE HOLIDAY HUSSY

Copyright ©2019 by Merry Farmer

Cover design by Erin Dameron-Hill (the miracle-worker)

ASIN: B083TQ2R7H

Paperback ISBN: 9798602364026

Click here for a complete list of other works by Merry Farmer.

If you'd like to be the first to learn about when the next books in the series come out and more, please sign up for my newsletter here: http://eepurl.com/RQ-KX

❀ Created with Vellum

CHAPTER 1

S omerset, England – December, 1815

COLD. LADY ALICE MARLOWE WAS FREEZING COLD and huddled in the corner of her seat in the hired carriage that bumped and jostled along the frozen lane, heading toward Holly Manor. She could barely feel her fingers, and her toes had long since gone numb. It didn't matter how tightly she pulled her shawl around her, the threadbare thing simply wasn't thick enough to provide adequate protection against the chill, December air.

"Stop fidgeting," Alice's father, Lord James Marlowe, the Earl of Stanhope, growled on the seat across from her. "You're making my head ache."

"Y-yes, F-father," Alice whispered through chattering teeth.

1

Her father looked just as cold as she did, but everything Alice knew about him told her he would rather die than admit to it. James Marlowe never admitted to anything. He refused to admit that his lands were in shambles because of his mismanagement. He refused to admit that, with only three daughters to his name, his title was on the verge of passing to his brother, Alice's delightful Uncle Richard. He refused to admit that the three marriages he'd arranged for his daughters at the house party at Hadnall Heath, home of Lord Rufus and Lady Caroline Herrington, were bad ones. And he most certainly refused to admit that Alice's younger sister, Imogen, had run off with Lord Thaddeus Herrington to avoid marrying her father's choice of groom.

"I said stop fidgeting," he snapped, grimacing at Alice without a shred of compassion for the cold. "Women should be invisible except when a man needs them to do their duty."

Alice gulped. "Yes, Father," she said, lowering her head.

"This spate of temper on your part is disgusting," he went on as though she had protested instead of meekly obeyed. "Count Fabian Camoni is an excellent match. His fame as a designer of gardens is known throughout England and the continent. And as soon as the mess Bonaparte has created in Italy is resolved, he will possess vast lands in Tuscany, which I understand are incredibly profitable."

Alice bit her tongue, knowing that anything she said would be taken the wrong way. Her father was desperate for money and the appearance that he was a man of importance and influence. Imogen had failed to help his cause by eloping with Lord Thaddeus, her older sister, Lettuce, had been married off to a wealthy but miserly merchant who had surprised them all by declaring he would take his bride and his fortune off to America without so much as a cent for their father, and so the entire burden of fulfilling their father's aims had landed squarely on Alice's shoulders.

He rubbed his hands together, but whether at the thought of the money he stood to gain through Alice's marriage or to ward off the cold, Alice didn't know. "Christmas is the perfect time to solidify this alliance," he went on. "It's a time of giving gifts and generosity. Not only will your groom give me the dowry price we agreed on, I'm certain I can squeeze more gold out of him. The fact that his mother remarried the Duke of Bolton is merely icing on the Christmas pudding. Bolton is dripping with money, and I have it on good authority that he's generous with his friends. This entire Christmas house party proves it."

"I thought the party was to celebrate the wedding," Alice said carefully. The last thing she wanted was to give her father the impression that she was blissfully going along with his plans. In fact, if she could have wrenched open the door and thrown herself out into the cold and barren landscape to avoid the whole thing, she would have.

Her father glared at her. "Arrogant chit," he hissed. "This endeavor is not about you."

Alice's eyes widened a fraction. Her own wedding was not about her? But of course, it wasn't. Her father would have required a heart to understand that marriages were supposed to be about love and companionability. They were supposed to contain passion, or at least mild attraction. And it wasn't as though she found Count Camoni unattractive. He'd been the prize catch of the house party with his rugged good looks and the aura of fame that surrounded him. Half of the young ladies at the party had flocked to him, gazing with open admiration at his broad shoulders and muscular frame, honed from all of the gardening work he did as part of his designs. They'd sighed over his blue eyes and blonde hair, which was unfashionably long, but glorious all the same. It wasn't his appearance or even his manners that filled Alice with dread and melancholy, it was the fact that she'd had no choice at all in the match. That and the fact that she hadn't seen him once since becoming engaged to him and had only had two letters in the five months since then.

"You will do your duty," her father went on in a lecturing tone. "After your marriage on Christmas Day, you will spread your legs eagerly for your husband so that he can get you with child as quickly as possible. An heir is the best way to ensure our families are entangled for all time."

Alice blushed with embarrassment at the mention of the marriage bed. She wasn't ignorant of those things, not after the Herrington's house party and the little souvenir she and her sisters had taken home and split between them. She wasn't even averse to them either. Part of her was exceptionally curious about matters of intimacy. But the thought of going to bed with Count Camoni because it was her duty, the idea that there was no point to the act but to produce an heir so that her father could sink his claws into Count Camoni's wealth, left her cold. Or perhaps that was merely the chill in the air.

Her father crossed his arms tightly and sank back into his seat, staring sullenly out the window at the frosty, Somerset countryside. The deep lines on his face hinted he had lapsed into thought and calculations about how he could increase his own fortunes. Alice waited, holding her breath, until she was relatively certain he wasn't paying attention to her any longer. Then she reached into the small satchel sitting on the seat beside her and drew out a book.

It wasn't a whole book. In fact, it was a third of one. When she and her sisters had discovered *The Secrets of Love* in a locked chest at the Herrington house party, it had felt as though they'd won a hunt for treasure. The volume contained everything any young woman could ever have wanted to know about the facts and fancies of love. Unlike most of the chaste and sedate books on the subject she had read before, *The Secrets of Love* contained vivid descriptions of the most sensual acts, interspersed between advice on how to find and keep a lover. Alice and her sisters had read the book so many times immediately after the house party that the spine had cracked. When each of their marriages were arranged and it became evident that the three of them would be split up, possibly never to see each other again, they'd divided the book in three, each of them taking a section.

Alice's middle section had no bindings, and it'd been all she could do to keep the pages from being damaged. She took one last peek at her father, and when she was certain he was distracted, she opened it to the chapter where she'd left off reading the night before. She already had most of the words memorized, but there was comfort in reading them again.

"*Love does not come with a sudden burst, like a man spending himself too soon only to fade and lose interest. It should unfold gradually, like a flower. First comes attraction, then intrigue, then titillation. Just as a lover undresses one article of clothing at a time or a gift is unwrapped bit by bit, the experience should be savored. By drawing out the process of love and reveling in each moment as it comes, passion and pleasure are increased, making the final blossoming all the more enjoyable.*"

Alice sighed, warming from the inside out. She could only imagine what it would be like to undress slowly for a lover, to make love the way she would savor a piece of cake instead of harshly lying back and parting her legs, like her father seemed to think she should do. Whoever the author of *The Secrets of Love* was, she—and Alice and her sisters were convinced the author was a woman—knew what a woman's heart longed for. And if there was one thing Alice's heart longed for, it was—

"What is that mangy pile of rubbish you're reading?" Her father snapped her out of her thoughts.

"It's nothing," Alice said with a gulp, slamming the pages closed and pushing the book back into her satchel before her father could read any of it.

"Don't you lie to me, you useless girl," he father growled.

"It's an instructional manual." Alice scrambled for an answer her father would believe and that wouldn't result in him taking the book from her. "About the duties of marriage. Lettuce, Imogen, and I were all given a copy after our engagements." It was marginally true, but Alice held her breath all the same.

"Who gave it to you?" her father asked, suspicion narrowing his eyes.

Alice had to lie. "Uncle Richard. He said it would improve our immortal souls."

Her father continued to glare, but he didn't comment. If there was anyone in the world that he feared, it was his younger brother. Uncle Richard was an army officer and a commanding presence. Her father didn't dare say a cross word against him.

"It's useless for women to read," he grumbled.

"There's no point in improving what cannot be improved, and anything else is frivolous waste. But never mind. We're here."

Blessedly, the carriage rolled to a stop in front of an enormous house. Alice hadn't realized they'd crossed onto the grounds of Holly Manor, but as she looked out when a footman raced down to open the carriage door, she was amazed by what she saw. The house itself was only fifty years old, but it had a gravity to it. At that moment, however, it was decorated for Christmas, with candles in the windows, boughs of pine and the holly that gave the estate its name strewn over the main door and front-facing windows, and cheery red bows adorning all.

Alice's father exited the carriage without looking back at her. Alice had to wait for the footman to hand her down. The rush of icy air that swirled around her made her teeth chatter, but the short line of Count Camoni's family and step-family waiting for them near the front door promised warmth to come.

"Hurry along, girl," her father growled, marching up the gravel path that crunched under his feet. He headed straight for the Duke of Bolton himself. "Good day, Your Grace." He smiled as though the world were filled with sunshine and light, as though he were a man prone to smiling.

"Lord Stanhope," the duke greeted him in return. "Welcome to our home. I trust you had a pleasant journey?"

"It was excellent," her father lied.

He continued his conversation with the duke, oblivious to all else, including Alice making her way toward the line of people at the front door, her limbs stiff with cold.

"This must be Lady Alice," a matronly woman came forward to greet her with an eager smile. Alice assumed at once that she was the duchess, Count Camoni's mother. "Oh dear, you look chilled through. Do come inside."

"Y-your grace." Alice managed a painful curtsy as she approached the woman. A second, much younger woman stood behind her, smiling at Alice with eager eyes. Behind her stood Count Camoni himself.

Alice nearly stumbled at the shock of seeing her betrothed again after so long. He was taller than she remembered, his shoulders broader and the power radiating from him stronger. He smiled at her as though she were a tasty morsel newly arrived for him to devour. Everything *The Secrets of Love* had taught her about the ways a man looked at a woman he wanted rushed back to her and she quivered on the inside, and not from fear.

"Georgette and I will have you warm and cozy in no time," the duchess went on.

The other young woman, Georgette, rushed to Alice's side, putting an arm around her and drawing her toward the house. "Goodness, you are cold," she said, then added, "I'm Lady Georgette Farnsworth. The duke is my father and your fiancé, Count Camoni, is my step-brother."

"Oh," Alice said, too overwhelmed to say more. She blinked at the attractive young woman, her rosy cheeks and her friendly eyes, gaped at the house as they passed through the front door and into an enormous hall decorated with exquisite artwork and suits of armor, and caught her breath as Georgette escorted her into a parlor across the hall where a cheery blaze crackled in a festively-decorated hearth. Everything around her was beautiful and expensive, and the people who flooded into the parlor with them were lofty and well-mannered. Alice knew in an instant that she was in well over her head. And that was before Count Camoni approached her.

SHE WAS EVERY BIT AS LOVELY AS HE REMEMBERED her to be. The moment Fabian laid eyes on his bride, he recalled all the reasons he had been so amenable to accepting her father's suggestion of marriage that summer. Alice was like a breath of fresh, spring air in, well, December. Although, she did look frozen through as his step-sister led her to the fireplace in the Forest Parlor. The cold had brought bright pink to her otherwise pale cheeks, and if he wasn't mistaken, the buttons standing out under the fabric of her too-thin bodice weren't buttons at all. He would never understand ladies' fashion and the inadequacy of the fabrics used these days. Alice should have been wearing a pelisse at the very least.

It had only begun to dawn on him that perhaps it

wasn't Alice's intention to dress so scantily and that, in fact, something else was behind the too-light clothing she wore, judging by the way she huddled near the fire, looking as though she might weep with relief, when Lord Stanhope stepped up to his side.

"Count Camoni," he said in an irritatingly ingratiating voice. "How nice to see you again."

Fabian dragged his attention away from his bride to accept his soon-to-be father-in-law's outstretched hand. "Lord Stanhope," he said, the feeling that Lord Stanhope's outstretched hand was asking for money settling over him. "I'm glad to see you and Lady Alice have arrived safely."

"I've delivered her into your hands, sir," Lord Stanhope said with a sly smile. "I trust the wedding will take place soon and we can settle on the bride price."

Fabian blinked in shock at the abruptness of Lord Stanhope's words. If it weren't for the fact that he truly did find Alice to be everything he wanted in a woman, he never would have entered into any sort of agreement to attach himself to the man. "Everything is in order," he answered without a smile. "But if you will excuse me, I would like to greet my bride."

"Yes, yes. You do that," Lord Stanhope said, thumping him on the back when he turned toward Alice.

Fabian frowned over his shoulder as he crossed the room. He caught the eye of his step-brother, Lord Matthew Farnsworth. The two were roughly the same age and had gotten along famously from the moment

Fabian's mother had married Matthew's father. They exchanged a look of brotherly knowing before Fabian reached the fireside and Alice.

"Lady Alice," Fabian greeted his vision of loveliness with a warm smile. "It is a joy and a pleasure to see you again."

To Fabian's disappointment, Alice glanced down, dipping into a short, polite curtsy before saying, "My lord," with all the disinterest of a child forced to sit through a particularly dull sermon.

Fabian's brow twitched as he scrambled to think of something more inviting to say. "I'm happy to see you looking so well. I thought the summer sun was becoming to you, but the coziness of a winter fire does just as much justice to your beauty."

She was silent, not meeting his eyes, shaking slightly, but whether from the cold or from something more sinister, Fabian couldn't tell. At last, she mumbled, "You are too kind."

Fabian's initial enthusiasm flattened to wary concern. "Are you well?" he asked. "You look a bit cold. Perhaps the journey was too taxing for you?"

"I am perfectly well, my lord." She snapped her eyes up to meet his with a look of tight frustration. Her hands clutched the satchel she carried to the point where her knuckles went white.

Worry took over entirely from the eagerness Fabian had felt while watching her carriage roll up the drive.

Something was wrong, but he couldn't imagine what it was. Unless....

"Please forgive me for not writing more often," he said in a quieter, more intimate voice. "I have had quite a few commissions to design winter gardens and greenhouses all across England this autumn. And the business of my father's family's estate in Tuscany has preoccupied me to an unforgivable degree. I swear, I will make it up to you by lavishing you with attention during this holiday party, before and after our marriage." He added a mischievous flicker of his eyebrows on the off chance that a hint of sensuality would thaw her icy demeanor.

"As you wish, my lord," she muttered, glancing down.

Fabian opened his mouth to say more, but he couldn't think of a blasted thing to say. Ladies usually adored him, though it was awkward to even think it. Apparently, he had a combination of good looks, good fortune, and exoticism that sent female hearts fluttering. Alice's was the only heart he cared to make flutter since the house party that summer, though. She'd been so free and curious then. Now he wasn't certain who she was.

"Perhaps," he began slowly, glancing to Georgette, "you would like to retire to the room we have prepared for you?" He lifted his eyebrows with the question. "There you might warm yourself by a fire or under layers of down quilts."

At last, she looked up at him with a measure of gratitude. "Thank you, my lord. That would be nice."

"Come along," Georgette said, looping an arm

around Alice's waist and nudging her forward. "I'll show you where you will be staying. I made certain Mama assigned you a room overlooking the garden. It's decorated in splendid fashion for the season."

Fabian stepped aside and watched as Georgette walked Alice out of the room. Lord Stanhope paused in the middle of what looked like an invasive conversation with the duke to stare at Georgette with open interest. He went so far as to absent-mindedly wipe his mouth, as if spotting a tasty morsel. Fabian kept his smile in place until Alice and Georgette disappeared around the corner, then let it drop into a troubled scowl. Lord Stanhope could be a problem if he latched onto Georgette.

"I thought you said Lady Alice was agreeable," Matthew said, stepping up beside him and tugging his thoughts back to his initial problem.

"She is," Fabian told him with a frown. "At least, she was this summer in Shropshire."

"Something must have happened between then and now," Matthew speculated, fingering the holly that decorated the mantel over the fire.

Fabian hummed, considering that. "I really shouldn't have been so distant with her once the engagement was settled."

"What could you have done?" Matthew shrugged. "You've been in high demand for over a year now, though why people hire a half-Italian to design gardens for them is beyond me." He grinned.

Fabian smiled at his friend's teasing. "Designing

gardens is a fair sight better than idling around, waiting for your father to die so you can become a duke."

Matthew laughed and nodded toward his father. "The old man isn't going to keel over any time soon. Your mother has infused him with new life."

Fabian arched a brow warily. "I'd rather not know what my mother gets up to behind closed doors." He shifted his stance, studying his mother and the duke with a thoughtful look all the same. "They may have the right way of things, though."

"How do you mean?" Matthew asked.

Fabian crossed his arms and rubbed his chin. "Your father put on quite a show to woo my mother. I never had a chance to do the same with Lady Alice."

"And all women love to be wooed," Matthew added.

"They do. And perhaps that's why Lady Alice was so cold just now. Perhaps the key thing is for me to spend the next few days before the wedding truly wooing her, making her feel special."

"Of course." Matthew laughed as if it were obvious. "You need to fall prostrate at her feet and worship the ground she walks on. You need to show her that you want to marry her because she is a goddess and you want to be in her temple at all times." He added a ribald wink to his comment.

"I wouldn't mind pouring out daily libations on the altar of her inner sanctum," Fabian agreed, equally lascivious.

"So do you know what you're going to do to win her?" Matthew asked.

Fabian glanced to the side, out the window, to spot the greenhouse he was in the middle of redesigning as an overdue wedding gift for his mother. "I have a few ideas," he said. "All it will take is a little plotting and a little magic."

CHAPTER 2

*I*t took Alice what felt like an eternity to warm up after Georgette showed her to the beautiful and lavish room that was to be hers for the first part of her stay at Holly Manor. The bed was piled sumptuously with down-filled quilts, and a cheery fire danced in the grate. Georgette even had one of the housemaids send up piping-hot tea to warm her from the inside. Between the cheery surroundings and kindness with which she'd been treated, Alice's spirits almost rose.

Until Georgette said, "It will be such a treat to have you as an almost-sister, once you and Fabian are married. He's not actually my brother, but he is so kind and jolly that it seems like it. Everyone has been thrilled that he will be married at last. We've all been blessing your father's name for arranging the union."

The smile that had worked its way onto Alice's face

dropped. "Yes, my father has been quite keen on the match."

Georgette continued to smile as she helped herself to one of the biscuits on the tea tray. "Your father seems like a wise and thoughtful man. It surprises me that he hasn't married again."

Alice was grateful that she'd just set down her teacup. She would have spewed tea all over her would-be friend if she hadn't. "If you had spent any amount of time in my father's presence, you would understand why he remains unmarried," she said, debating whether it was safe to come right out and tell a new acquaintance all the horrors of which her father was capable.

"I will make it a point to attend to him, then," Georgette said. Before Alice could do more than widen her eyes in horror, she sped on with, "Now, if you will excuse me, we have more guests due to arrive, and I promised Papa and Lady Marie that I would play hostess."

Georgette finished her biscuit with a giggle of delight, then rushed for the door. She sent Alice one last smile before dashing out into the hall and shutting the door behind her.

Alice snapped her mouth closed without having a chance to warn Georgette to stay away from her father. Her shoulders slumped as she stared at the closed door. The young woman couldn't possibly have it in her head that her father would make a good match, could she? Georgette was the daughter of a duke. Her father was an earl, but he was easily double Georgette's age, and not even the title Countess of Stanhope was worth being married to a cruel and heartless man like him.

The fear that Georgette was on the verge of doing something awful lingered with Alice through the rest of the afternoon, during which she climbed into bed and napped until she was warm, and through a dull supper attended by over a dozen travel-weary guests who weren't in the mood for conversation. It niggled at the back of her mind through the night and was there with her when she woke and dressed the next morning.

She had firmly decided to take Georgette aside and explain the folly of her ways by breakfast the next morning. After fixing a plate of the finest pastries and meats she had ever seen, she deliberately took a seat by Georgette at the breakfast table.

"There is a matter of great importance that I must discuss with you," she began.

Georgette had only just turned away from her brother and glanced to Alice with a questioning look when Count Camoni stood from his place on the other side of the table and cleared his throat. The rest of the chattering guests quieted with astounding speed to listen to whatever he had to say.

"Ladies and Gentlemen, I would like to invite you to a special display of horticultural wonder in my mother's greenhouse this morning," he said.

A chorus of oohs and aahs sounded around the table. Alice didn't know any of the other guests, but they all clearly knew exactly who Count Camoni was. They all watched him with looks of admiration that bordered on worship. But what made Alice squirm in her chair was that Count Camoni watched her with the same near-worship. What stories had her father told him about her that inspired such misplaced affection toward her? It felt like yet another one of her father's traps that she was helpless to escape.

"This display is not only in honor of Christmastide," Count Camoni went on. "It is a tribute to my lovely bride, Lady Alice Marlowe."

He gestured across the table to her and Alice wanted to sink into the floor. Every eye at the table turned to her, scrutinizing her as the woman who managed to snatch the famous object of their adoration away from them. Worse still, near the head of the table, her father looked on with a smirk that was so self-satisfied it turned Alice's stomach and put her off her bacon.

But that wasn't the very worst of it. Her father's grin slid past Alice and landed firmly on Georgette, who returned the look with a smile and a nod. It was the most horrible set of circumstances she could possibly have found herself in. Count Camoni was still standing across the table from her, watching her, but his pleased smile had faded. Alice felt like a bloom that had failed to live up to his standards as he sat once more. She tried her best not to look at him as conversations resumed around the table. Saving Georgette was her first priority, though, not living up to whatever lies her father had told Count Camoni about her.

She turned to Georgette and opened her mouth to speak, but before she could get a word out, Count Camoni said, "I do hope you will enjoy the display this morning."

Alice felt as though he'd looped an arm around her middle and yanked her away from Georgette. Since Georgette had leaned close to her brother to whisper something to him, she was forced to face her fiancé and answer, "Yes, I'm certain it will be lovely."

She attempted to turn back to Georgette, but Count Camoni went on. "I remember from the house party this summer that you have a particular fondness for dahlias, so I have incorporated quite a few in the display."

Alice blinked. "I'm surprised you remember."

"How could I forget?" he asked with a smile.

As handsome and warm as his smile was, it made her uncomfortable. It was too sensual, held too much promise. It was like a drop of honey placed in a trap to draw in a fly for the kill. The mad thought that her father had put him up to it hit her. Not that there was anything she could do to save herself. She was doomed to be nothing more than a pawn in her father's marital machinations.

"Lady Alice," the snowy-haired matron on her right interrupted the conversation Count Camoni was trying to have with her. "I understand that you attended Lord and Lady Herrington's infamous house party this past summer. What was that like?"

Alice could have wept with relief at being given the excuse to ignore Count Camoni without seeming rude.

She launched into a thorough description of the house party as her fiancé looked on, remaining silent. The matron, one of Georgette's aunts, nodded and smiled, laughing at all the right places, enjoying the story. Alice couldn't have been happier. It meant she didn't have to converse with, or even look at, Count Camoni for the rest of breakfast.

It did, however, mean that she wasn't given the chance to speak to Georgette to warn her not to give in to her father. So as soon as the company finished breakfast and made their way to the greenhouse, Alice did everything she could to avoid Count Camoni and her father to slip up to Georgette's side.

"Lady Georgette," she began once the two of them stepped through the wide doors at the back of one of the larger parlors to cross the dormant garden and make their way to the greenhouse, "I must speak with you on a matter of utmost importance, right away."

"That sounds exciting," Georgette said, looping her arm through Alice's and marching to the greenhouse at a brisk pace. "It's about Fabian, isn't it?" she asked with a conspiratorial wink. "The way he was looking at you all through breakfast gave me palpitations. You're such a lucky young woman."

Alice couldn't help but cringe at her new friend's words. She was as unlucky as could be to find herself firmly snared and on the verge of being married to a man she barely knew. "It's not my marriage that concerns me at present," she said as they stepped through the door into the greenhouse.

As soon as they entered the humid, verdant space, Alice lost track of what she was saying. She'd seen many greenhouses before, but nothing half as grand or beautiful as the space she'd stepped into. All around her, the scent of rich earth and greenery filled the air. Blooms and blossoms from all parts of the globe were arranged in neat displays that served both a practical use and pleased the eye. But in the middle of it all, a wide circle had been marked out that was surrounded by chairs. Several tables that looked like gears in one of the newfangled machines that was taking over industry surrounded a glass armonica, which was being played by an artistic-looking man with a somber expression. On the outer edge of the circle, just in front of the chairs, a series of miniature fountains sprayed and danced in ever-changing patterns.

Alice gasped along with the rest of the guests at the sight. She dropped Georgette's arm and approached the central display with the wonder of a child. The man playing the armonica ended his song and began a haunting rendition of Bach's Christmas oratorio that had the hair standing up on the back of her neck.

She barely noticed when Count Camoni swept past her, strode around the back of the display, and stepped into the center by the armonica player's side. "Please, come closer," he said, looking right at her, though Alice had the feeling he was addressing everyone. "There's so much more to see."

Alice did as he asked, sitting in the chair at the front that he indicated. Georgette was suddenly the furthest thing from her mind. She clasped her hands in front of her and drank in the sight of the fountains, the sound of the armonica, and the wonder of it all.

"Ladies and gentlemen," Count Camoni said, a twinkle in his eyes. "I give you the dance of the dahlias."

He leaned to one side and turned a crank, all the while watching Alice with a smile. Instantly, the entire display came to life. The small, round tables began to move, rotating themselves, turning around each other, and swirling in one grand circle around Count Camoni, the armonica, and its player. A hundred, bright dahlias had been fixed to the table somehow, and as the whole thing turned, they appeared to be twirling and dancing, like village girls in bright skirts at a festival.

Alice's breath caught in her throat at the sight. It was magical in so many ways, and judging by the way Count Camoni watched her, hers was the only reaction he cared about. Had he truly made the entire display just for her?

That beautiful thought was squashed a moment later as her gaze slipped to the side and she spotted her father taking a seat beside Georgette. He leaned scandalously close to her and whispered something in Georgette's ear that made her giggle.

Dread and rage filled Alice, dampening any enthusiasm she had for Count Camoni's display. She wasn't ignorant enough not to guess that her father had his sights firmly set on Georgette now. Georgette was the ideal prey for him. Her father was rich, she was young and pretty, and with his daughters all married off, she would make exactly the sort of wife he craved. Alice absolutely could not let it happen.

The armonica player finished his song and a hearty round of applause broke out among the guests. Georgette and Alice's father clapped as well. Alice merely swallowed, writhing with anxiety.

"There's much more to see," Count Camoni announced, coming around the display once more to stand before it. "Please feel free to wander about the greenhouse to see everything I've done, at my mother's request. Though she is not the only woman I hope I have impressed today."

As soon as the other guests rose from their seats and began to mill around the vast greenhouse, Alice jumped to her feet as well. But she didn't turn to Count Camoni, not even when he took a step toward her. Instead, she dashed to the side, desperate to stop her father from whisking Georgette away.

FABIAN'S MOUTH HUNG OPEN, THE CONVERSATION he'd been about to start with Alice fading before he could say a word. She leapt from her chair as though stung by a bee and sped away from him. His shoulders dropped as he watched her dodge around a few guests and chairs, heading for her father and Georgette.

"Count Camoni, that was amazing," Lord Harrow,

one of his mother's guests, rushed to speak to him before he could chase after Alice.

"Thank you, my lord." Fabian shook the man's hand, glancing over his shoulder so that he could keep an eye on Alice. She had been stopped by Lord George Percival, one of Matthew's friends, who was staying for the week. George seemed particularly eager to speak to her.

"I must commission you to redesign my greenhouse," Lord Harrow went on. "Although I hear your services are in extremely high demand."

"I am fortunate to have gained a reputation for horti-cultural excellence," Fabian said with a nod. His frown deepened as the conversation between Alice and George continued. Alice seemed overly emotional and gestured toward one of the more secluded paths within the greenhouse.

"So what do you say?" Lord Harrow went on. "I can pay you whatever you ask to update all of my gardens."

George said something, Alice nodded, and the two of them started down the path.

"If you will excuse me for a moment, my lord," Fabian said distractedly, stepping away from Lord Harrow.

He didn't see how the man reacted. Urgency pushed him to follow Alice, and a hot streak of jealousy demanded he discover what the connection was between her and George.

The greenhouse was extensive, but the wonders it held weren't enough to hold most of the guests there for any length of time. At least half of the company had already headed back to the house by the time he traced Alice's steps and found her standing at the end of a long row of particularly bushy ferns. George was nowhere in sight, but that didn't mean the bastard hadn't ducked through the greenery to make himself scarce. Alice darted a worried look around, as if in the hope George had made it to safety before his appearance.

"Is there something I can help you with?" Fabian asked, approaching Alice like a panther stalking his prey.

"N-no, my lord," she said, clasping her hands in front of her and looking down. She bit her lip in a manner that suggested guilt.

"What happened to your friend?" he asked in a flat voice, moving to within feet of her.

"I don't know," Alice sighed, letting down a fraction of her guard. "I have to...I was trying...my father...." She gave up whatever she was trying to say with a heavy breath, then glanced warily up at him, as if just realizing he was standing too close.

A thousand questions flashed through Fabian's mind. Was something illicit going on between her and George? At the house party, she'd been sweet to the point of girlishness, but a lot could have happened in five months. Perhaps she and George had met and become much closer than they should have. Fabian knew that plenty of married women took lovers when they were bored or felt neglected by their husbands. Perhaps Alice had gotten a head start on cuckolding him.

"How did you like the display?" he asked, pulling himself to his full height and scrutinizing her to see if she showed any signs of infidelity.

"It was lovely," she answered, glancing anxiously around, as though her lover would pop out of the ferns at any moment. "It's just that...."

She continued her search but not her words.

Fabian decided to face the problem head-on. "Marriage is a daunting business," he said. "It would be a shame to enter one ill-advisedly or to start off on the wrong foot."

To his surprise, she turned her full attention to him and said, "Yes. Exactly. One's choice of partner can bring joy or utter misery, which is why...." Again, she swallowed the end of her sentence, her cheeks flushing.

Fabian clenched his jaw. She was hiding something from him. It had to be a lover. She wouldn't have been so short with him if she hadn't given her heart to another. Practically every woman he'd ever met had fancied him, or at least treated him with the respect his fame brought with it, except those who were already in love with someone else.

"Your father strikes me as a man of exceptionally good taste," he said, trying another angle. Lord Stanhope was the one who had suggested the two of them marry, after all. Perhaps he knew about Alice's affair and was in a hurry to palm her off on some unsuspecting suitor.

As if to prove him right, her eyes went wide and she gazed up at him suspiciously. "My father never did anything selflessly in his life, and this...this is beyond the pale."

Fabian's frown darkened. From the sound of things, Alice didn't want to marry him at all. He could see the trepidation in her expression. It only seemed to prove she wanted someone else entirely.

"You think so?" he asked in stilted tones.

She didn't answer. He didn't give her a chance to. Whether it was his wounded pride or some other, darker force, he couldn't let her insolence go unchecked. He stepped toward her, scooping an arm around her waist and tugging her flush against him. With all the power of a conquering general, he slanted his mouth over hers, kissing her mercilessly.

Her body stiffened against his for a moment before relaxing as a deep moan sounded from her throat. His lips devoured hers, and when she parted them, he thrust his tongue along hers, tasting and exploring and taking what he wanted from her. He swore he could feel a shudder pass through her as she clutched his sides, digging her fingertips into his flesh.

As forcefully as their kiss had begun, it was like heaven. She submitted to him fully, letting him ravish her in a way that had him hard in an instant. He shifted one hand to cradle her ample breast, rubbing his thumb over her nipple until it was a taut peak. She whimpered under the onslaught of his mouth but didn't try to pull away.

Only a hussy would let a man who wasn't her husband kiss her so thoroughly. An innocent maid would shriek and run screaming from a display of passion like that. She had to have a lover. That was why she'd been so cold to him.

Those thoughts sparked through him in an instant. Before he could act on them or say anything, though, Lord Stanhope stepped suddenly toward them from the end of the aisle of ferns.

"There you are," he said, a note of triumph in his voice.

Sense and embarrassment closed in on Fabian and he let go of Alice, stepping respectfully away from her. What had he been thinking to kiss her like she was a strumpet for hire?

He'd been thinking she *was* a strumpet for hire, of course.

"Lord Stanhope. Forgive me," he said, bowing to the man.

To his surprise, instead of telling him off or demanding the wedding take place that instant to preserve his daughter's honor, he merely grinned. The expression sent a chill down his back, especially when he glanced past Fabian to nod to his daughter. "Well done," he said. "I knew you were a good, obedient girl underneath it all."

Fabian opened his mouth to ask what the devil that meant, but Lord Stanhope stepped around the corner, disappearing as quickly as he'd appeared. He frowned, shaking his head, then turned back to Alice.

His heart dropped to his stomach at what he found.

Alice stood with her shoulders slumped and her head bowed, the picture of defeat and misery. Her cheeks were bright pink with shame, and even though he couldn't see them fully, he had a feeling her eyes were brimming with tears. The pitiful sight had him questioning every conclusion he had just come to.

"I'm sorry," she whispered, sniffled, then launched forward, pushing past him. She clapped a hand to her mouth as she turned the corner in the opposite direction her father had gone.

Fabian was left standing alone, a puzzled frown growing deeper on his brow. Something was terribly wrong. Did Alice have a lover or not? What had her father meant by calling her obedient? Was he walking into some sort of trap that was closing in around him? He couldn't make heads nor tails of the whole thing. All he knew was that he had to get to the bottom of the mystery, and the sooner, the better.

CHAPTER 3

*A*lice was desperate. Try as she did through the afternoon, she couldn't catch Georgette alone to warn her about her father. Her father had most certainly decided Georgette was the perfect prey...or rather, the perfect wife. Alice stood by helplessly as he courted and flattered Georgette through an afternoon of parlor games, and as he chose a seat beside her at supper. Every time Alice tried to intervene, something had happened or someone had drawn her into a conversation about how delighted she must be to wed the famous Count Camoni.

Count Camoni was her other problem. The way he'd kissed her in the greenhouse had driven all sense straight from her mind. His body had enveloped her with heat and power. His lips and tongue had drawn a passion up from her soul that she hadn't known existed. It could have been August rather than December for all the heat that pulsed through her as he held her, caressing her curves. An ache had formed in an unmentionable part of her body with his kiss. That ache renewed all through the afternoon whenever she spotted Count Camoni watching her. And he seemed to be watching her constantly with a slight frown that left her breathless, with too many emotions to count.

But Count Camoni was a distraction she couldn't afford. Not when the future happiness of a nice young woman was in danger. Alice lay awake that night, tossing and turning and fretting over what she should and could do. Her bedsheets tangled around her legs and her shoulders bunched with tension as she mulled over the problem. It didn't help one bit that her concern for Georgette quickly became mingled with memories of Count Camoni kissing her. She could still taste him. His scent still filled her senses. The memory of the way he'd touched her breast was so powerful that she fondled herself to see if she could recreate the sensation.

"It's no use," she growled at last, kicking off the covers and twisting to sit. "I have to do something."

She rose from the bed with a determined huff, crossing to the table and lighting the lamp that waited there. With that light, she found her dressing gown and threw it over her shoulders. Then she fetched the lamp and tip-toed out into the hall.

Holly Manor was silent in slumber. Not a soul was awake, not even the servants. Alice crept down the hall, studying the doors she passed with a frown. Her father had been given a room on a separate hall, but there was no telling who might be behind the doors on her hall. She breathed a slight sigh of relief when she reached the stairs and climbed up a floor. Georgette had told her where the family quarters were located during the brief tour she'd given a group of guests the day before, and she'd pointed out which room was hers when they were outside briefly. Alice was confident she could locate her new friend's room, steal in, and give her the warning that was so desperately needed.

Once she was in the family wing, she stole along, counting doors and making calculations in her head. Georgette's room had to be the third one on the right. She reached the door, contemplated knocking, but decided that was too risky. Instead, she tested the handle.

The door was unlocked and swung open with a slight creak. The room beyond was dark and the curtains were closed to keep the heat from the embers left in the fireplace contained. With a squeeze of triumph in her chest, Alice hurried inside, then turned and shut the door behind her.

"Georgette," she whispered, barely audible.

She was greeted by the deep sound of someone breathing in their sleep under the pile of quilts on the bed. She would have to be louder to wake her friend.

"Georgette," she called, still in a whisper.

She inched closer to the bed as the breathing hitched and the pile of quilts stirred. Relief spilled through her, and she hurried all the way to the side of the bed, setting the lamp on the bedside table.

"Georgette, I must speak with you at once. I—" Alice sucked in a breath as a large form, far larger than Georgette was, twisted under the quilts to face her. "George—"

She yelped and clapped a hand to her mouth as the bedcovers were pushed back and Count Camoni squinted up at her in the dim light. There was a moment of confusion in his sleepy eyes before it resolved into ire.

"George?" he said, his voice louder than Alice wanted it to be. She tried to shush him by touching a finger to her lips and glancing over her shoulder, but he sat and demanded a second time, "George? What is the meaning of this?"

Terror roiled in Alice's gut, not the least of which was because, as he sat, the bedcovers slumped to reveal Count Camoni's powerful, naked chest. The lamplight was more than enough for her to see the definition in his muscles and the light hair that dusted his chest. His arms were a sight to behold as well, with a firmness that brought the ache instantly back to her core.

"This is a mistake," she whispered, barely able to form the words as she drank in the sight of his body.

"I'll say it is," he growled. "So you thought you could sneak into your lover's room for an assignation right under my nose?"

"I—" Alice barely heard his question. He shifted the way he was sitting and a stretch of his naked thigh poked out from the bedcovers, hinting that he wore nothing at all to bed.

"Is this why you've been so cold to me these last few days?" he demanded, glowering at her.

Alice dragged her eyes up from his body, but she couldn't manage to shut her mouth as she stared at him. A riot of feeling played havoc with her senses. His expression was truly terrifying. Like he might punish her for her wickedness. But that didn't strike her as an entirely bad thing. The words of her section of *The Secrets of Love* rushed back to her. "*Sometimes submission is the most glorious way to move a romance forward. Embrace his mastery of you and pleasures you have never known will be opened to you.*"

He was still glaring at her and she hadn't answered. She blinked, determined to do something about that. "George?" she asked, taking a deep breath that caused an alarming friction between her nipples and the fabric of her nightgown.

"Yes," Count Camoni said, narrowing his eyes. "You know, the man whose bed you tried to hop into? The man you've likely been dallying with all these months of our engagement?"

She didn't have the first clue what he was talking about. "No." She shook her head. "I only meant that...I have to warn...she can't marry him or...." Why couldn't she think or form words?

A flash of uncertainty filled Count Camoni's eyes, although it could have been the play of shadows from the dim light. "What does he give you that I cannot?" he asked.

Alice gaped for a moment, scrambling to decipher his meaning. He had to be referring to her father. She didn't know any other men. "He's...I suppose he's provided for me," she said with a frown of confusion.

"Provided for you, has he?" Count Camoni seemed indignant at her perfectly normal response.

"Yes?" She shivered, certain she'd put every foot wrong.

"I suppose he sees to your physical needs as well," Count Camoni went on in a bitter voice.

Alice bit her lip, knowing she wouldn't say the right thing. "Isn't that what he's supposed to do?"

As she'd predicted, it was the wrong thing to say. Count Camoni looked downright livid. She expected him to start shouting and to either order her from the room or smack her, like her father sometimes did when he was in a particularly foul mood.

But he shocked her by growling, "We'll just see about that," and surging toward her.

She barely had time to gulp a breath before Count Camoni captured her and twisted her so that she lay on her back in his bed. He closed a hand possessively over her hip and swooped down to punish her mouth with a kiss that overwhelmed her. His lips played aggressively with hers, and when she parted hers just a little, he took full advantage, plunging his tongue in to plunder her.

She moaned deep in her throat, feeling as though the

world had tipped off-balance. He was so powerful and demanding. Her lips felt tender and bruised within moments, but she didn't want him to stop. She arched against him, but gasped when the fullness of his naked body pressed back against her.

"Are you so voracious that you don't care who your lover is as long as they pleasure you?" he rumbled above her. His large hand reached down her leg to gather the hem of her nightgown, tugging it up. "If you want it, I'll give it to you."

Alice's mind reeled. Through her shock and fear came the realization that she did want it. She wasn't sure what it was, but if it had anything to do with the way he caressed her thigh, teasing his fingers toward her aching sex, then yes, that was exactly what she wanted.

"Does he make you feel like this?" Count Camoni asked on, yanking her nightgown up over her hips, then spreading his hand across her belly. It didn't stay there for long. He traced her navel with one finger, then slid his hand down to the thatch of curls between her legs. He didn't stop there either, His fingers delved into her folds, stroking her overheated sex.

Alice tried to say something, anything, but all that came out was a sensual sigh. Sharp bolts of pleasure, like nothing she'd ever experienced before, coursed through her as he traced her entrance with his fingers, then thrust one slowly inside of her. Her eyes went wide at the invasion and she couldn't seem to catch her breath.

"I should have known a hussy like you would be wet

and panting for it," he growled, though there was something warm and teasing in his tone, something beyond anger. "I bet you like cock. I bet you lie awake at night, abusing yourself and dying for a big, thick, hard cock ramming into you until you come so hard you cry."

Alice tried to answer, but all that came out was a strangled cry as he added a second finger to his ministrations. Heaven help her, but she liked it and she wanted more.

"Does George have a big cock?" he demanded. Her overtaxed mind had no idea what he was talking about. "Is it as big as this?"

He drew his hand away from her, finding her hand where it lay, limp and useless, on the bed beside her, and pulling it toward him. She gasped as he pressed her hand to his cock. Not only did the gesture prove that yes, he was fully naked, it answered the question he'd just asked her. He was enormous. Not that she had much to compare him with. His erect penis was hot and hard, like iron covered with soft leather, and as thick as a tree trunk. Well, perhaps not that thick, but it might as well have been.

He moved her hand so that she stroked him, which only emphasized his size and power.

"Do you like that?" he asked in a tense voice, his eyes blazing with fire in the feeble light of the lamp. "Do you want it in you?"

The very idea made Alice shudder with longing and fear. Certainly, something that size could never fit inside of her. But the only sound that came from her throat was an incoherent, "Ahmm."

He braced himself above her, studying her with narrowed eyes, his too-long hair hanging down and framing his face. It took Alice a few moments to realize she had continued stroking his erection, even after he moved his hand away.

"You're going to marry me," he said with a note of finality. "And when you do, I don't want you so much as looking at another man again."

Alice wasn't sure she'd ever be able to look at another man, not after what was happening to her just then.

"I want you screaming my name when you come from now on, do you hear me?"

She blinked up at him, only half understanding what he was demanding of her. "Yes?"

Her answer must not have been definitive enough for him. "My name," he repeated. "I want my name on your lips when you writhe with lust and demand satisfaction." When she didn't say anything, he went on with, "Say my name."

Alice's lips worked soundlessly for a moment. It was asking too much of her to form coherent thoughts when his body was pressed against hers and his cock rubbed against her hip. "Count Camoni?" she panted at last.

His expression darkened. "It's Fabian," he told her in a low rumble.

The sound made her shiver and squirm. "Fabian," she repeated.

He didn't look appeased. Not one bit. He moved to wedge the lower half of his body between her legs. "Say it like you mean it."

She couldn't imagine what he wanted from her. "Fabian?"

He growled, resting a hand on her belly for a moment before drawing it up to caress her breast. The way he squeezed and kneaded it, brushing his fingers over her nipple until it was a hard point, sent shoots of pleasure radiating through her. Then he pinched her nipple lightly and she cried out wordlessly at the heady combination of pleasure and pain.

"Say it," he demanded, increasing the pressure of his pinch until she squirmed, her sex on fire with need.

"Fabian," she gasped.

He released the pressure and returned to caressing and teasing her breast. It felt even better after the flash of pain. He took a moment to sweep his hands over her arms, arranging them over her head as though he were a sculptor and she was his clay. The position left her feeling open and vulnerable, and decidedly wicked.

"You have the body of a goddess," he said in sultry tones, stroking his hand along the curve of her neck and over her shoulder to tease and fondle her other breast. "It was made for fucking. No wonder you're such a harlot."

In the back of her mind, Alice thought that perhaps she should be offended by his words. Offense was the furthest thing from her mind, though. Especially when he rocked back so that he could use both hands to wrench her knees apart. The motion was so sudden and so carnal that she could barely catch her breath. He pushed her legs apart, knees bent, so that her sex yawned wide for him. Her body trembled as though she were terrified, but the sensation of liquid heat pulsing through her was anything but fear.

"Does he spread you like this?" Fabian asked, stroking her thighs in a way that made it impossible for Alice to pay attention to what he was saying. "Does he play with your cunny until it's dripping with your honey?"

He didn't give her a chance to answer. She couldn't have formed words as he brushed his fingers over her gaping sex anyhow. The pleasure was too amazing. He plunged his fingers inside of her, then spread her moisture up over her clitoris. It felt so good when he stroked and circled that part of her that she wanted to weep with the pleasure of it. If this was what *The Secrets of Love* meant by submitting, she was all for it.

"Come," he ordered her. "I want to watch your cunny throbbing with release." He continued to pleasure her with steady strokes. "I want you to call out my name as you shudder, knowing that I am the one doing this to you."

She was already startlingly close to doing exactly as he wanted. The coil of tension began to radiate with her coming orgasm, leaving her short of breath.

"And when you're finished coming, I'm going to fuck

you so deeply that you won't remember your own name, let alone the name of any other men."

That was all it took. Her body thundered into the most powerful orgasm she'd ever experienced, far more earth-shattering than anything she'd been able to coax out herself. And as the pleasure throbbed through her, she sighed, "Fabian. Dear God, Fabian."

A wicked smile spread across his face and a wolfish gleam lit his eyes. He surged forward, his body sliding over hers. The shift from icy cold air to his hot body covering her was delicious, but it was the sudden, merciless way he brought himself to her still throbbing entrance and pushed firmly inside of her that caused her to cry out without words.

It hurt. Dear heavens, it hurt. Like being torn in two from the inside. But the lingering pleasure of orgasm was also there, and the aggressive way he moved in and out of her, jerking his hips against her and grunting with each thrust, ignited something beyond the pain. She clenched her thighs over his and clung to him, digging her nails into his back, as he mated with her in a combination of fury and desperation.

Pleasure quickly eclipsed the pain, though he still felt impossibly huge inside of her, and a new set of sensations swept through her. He was wild and uncontrolled, like an animal with his mate. He needed her as his vessel and his anchor, she could feel it. His power was all hers, encompassing her, but with her as its source.

The sounds he made became unfettered, and a tension radiated from him as though something momentous were about to happen. His breathing became shallower, then turned to a tight cry of victory as his body tensed. His hips flexed against hers, and the sensation of warmth and completeness filled her as his seed spilled within her. She gasped as a second orgasm overtook her, milking him even as he sagged, his loose weight pressing down on her. The whole thing was glorious and strange, and left her bristling with the feeling that they'd abandoned reality altogether.

"You're mine," he purred, rolling to his side, then reaching for her and tucking her against him. He reached groggily for the bedcovers, closing them in a cocoon of heat and the scent of sweat and musk. "You're mine, and don't you forget it."

His voice grew groggy, and within moments, Alice had the feeling he'd fallen fast asleep. Her body ached and tingled with spent energy and amazement. Her sex stung with the loss of her virginity. Her lips were still swollen from his kisses, but she had yet to catch her breath. He was right. She was his. Unequivocally. And as mad and sudden as the whole thing had been, as used as her body felt, she wanted more. Much more.

CHAPTER 4

*F*abian would have been happy to awake
with the dawn chorus the next morning,
Alice soft and warm in his arms. He would have grinned
at his conquest from the night before, stretched, and run
his hands over Alice's naked body, arousing her to wake-
fulness. He would have wanted nothing more than to
greet the day by lazily making love to her, listening to her
signs of pleasure mingling with the whisper of the winter
wind against his window and her desperate moans as she
came. He would have loved to spend himself deep inside
of her, hoping his seed took hold to start the large family
he craved and knowing that anticipating their wedding
vows by a few days wouldn't matter in the long run.

What he actually felt as the cold light of morning
crept around the gaps between the curtains was a
profound sense of doom and guilt.

He shifted as subtly as he could, lifting his head to see if Alice was awake. Unsurprisingly, she was. Her body was tense against his and she stared straight forward at the wall. Fabian winced. He'd behaved like an utter brute with her the night before. Jealousy and the shock of being awakened without fully coming to his senses had made him crass. His stomach twisted at the memory of the things he'd said to her. He hoped he had just imagined half of them.

But worst of all, a few, gut-wrenching details of the way her body had felt as he plundered her, the way she had reacted to his invasion, had him doubting every assumption he'd made in anger. Women of experience and cunning didn't respond to lust the way Alice had.

"You...." He hesitated, mustering up the courage to go on. "You weren't seeking out George for an assignation last night, were you." It wasn't a question.

Alice blinked and twisted to her back, turning her head to face him. The shift brought her body into contact with his in a dozen arousing ways. He couldn't help his physical reaction to her, but he ignored it and focused on the confusion in her eyes.

"Who's George?" she asked.

Fabian's lips twitched into a smile even as the dread in his gut writhed like snakes. She was as sweet and lovely as she had been that summer, which was remarkable, all things considered. "George Percival?"

She blinked at him again, shaking her head slightly.

"The man you spoke to in the greenhouse after the display yesterday?"

A slight frown furrowed her brow before she sucked in a breath, the confusion clearing from her expression. "Is that what his name was? I was asking him if he'd seen which way Georgette went."

Like the blast of a cannon, it all made sense to Fabian. She hadn't said "George" when she entered his room in the middle of the night. She'd clearly said "Georgette", but he'd heard what he expected to hear. Alice was innocent of attempting to cuckold him under his mother's roof, days before their wedding. At least....

He cleared his throat. "Tell me plainly. Were you a virgin before last night?"

Alice's eyes popped wide. "Of course, I was," she said with equal parts indignation and shyness.

Fabian dropped his head in shame, grimacing. "I'm sorry," he said. "I'm so, so sorry. I was brutal with you. I let an imagined offense turn me into a beast. No woman should be introduced to pleasure that way."

Alice's cheeks went bright red and a gentle smile tilted the corners of her mouth. "I didn't mind," she said in a voice so low it was almost a whisper. "Well, it hurt for a moment, but it was quite thrilling. And pleasurable."

Fabian's cock jerked at her words. The beast that had ravaged her the night before roared within him, urging him to spread her legs and claim her as his all over again. "You liked it?" he asked, his words coming out with ridiculous vulnerability that formed a stark contrast with the smoldering heat in his groin. He closed a hand over one of her dazzlingly full breasts to feed the beast instead of his sheepishness.

Alice's smile grew as she drew in a breath, arching her back. "Does it make me a complete wanton if I did?" she asked.

"Yes," he answered, shifting closer to her and nudging her legs apart with one knee. "But as you are to be my wife, I will allow it."

He surged toward her, intent on kissing her until she was dizzy, but instead of turning into the pool of pliability she'd been during the night, she gasped, "Oh!" and sat up. The movement was so abrupt that her shoulder hit his jaw, knocking him firmly out of his cloud of lust.

"What?" he asked, sitting with her. His eyes honed in on her exposed breasts—gorgeous, heavy orbs that he instantly imagined himself kneading and suckling and even fucking until he came in a string of pearls around her neck—which she didn't bother to cover.

"Georgette," she said, her sweet face hardening into a mask of determination as she attempted to scoot through the tangled bedsheets to the side of the bed. "I have to find her. I have to warn her."

Fabian reached out, hooking his arm around her waist and tugging her flush against him. "You don't have to go anywhere at the moment," he said, raising his hands to fondle her breasts as he looked down at them over her shoulder. He shifted so that he sat with his back against the headboard and positioned Alice between his legs, his cock pressed tightly against her luscious backside.

She attempted to say something that came out as an incoherent sigh and tilted her head back. "I can't think when you do that."

"Good," he said, kneading her breasts with slightly more pressure. "I don't want you to think, I just want you to feel."

"But Georgette," she started, then gasped when he pinched her nipples. The gasp turned into a squeal. "Ooh, why do I like that so much when it hurts?"

Another surge of lust pounded through Fabian, and he jerked his hips against her backside. "Because it's not dangerous pain," he said. "You know I'm not trying to hurt you. A little sting only makes the pleasure better."

She made another incoherent sound that might have been agreement or a plea for him to give her more. The way she wiggled her backside against him certainly led him to believe she wanted him buried deep within her. But still she managed to form the words, "Georgette. I have to warn her not to trust—oh!"

Fabian bit her shoulder gently to stop her worry. Her breath came in tight pants and heat radiated from her. He slipped one hand from her breast, across her belly, and between her legs to test her. Sure enough, she was as wet as a rainstorm over the ocean.

"I'll tell you what," he purred against the side of her head. "I'm going to bend you forward and fuck your tight, wet pussy until we both come. Then I'll let you get up, dress, and go in search of Georgette to tell her whatever you want to."

She answered with a mewling sound, sucking in a breath as he rubbed her clit, and nodded.

The beast was back in command. Even if he'd wanted to, Fabian wasn't sure he could have waited. Sometimes long and slow was the way to go, but in that moment, fast and hard was right.

He tipped her forward until she spilled, head down, across the bunched quilts. Her body was loose and submissive as he lifted her hips and spread her legs. The sight of her so open and at his mercy, the slick, pink folds of her pussy gaping open for him, beckoning, was almost more than he could take. He positioned himself on his knees behind her, grasping her hips and jerking her back toward him.

He slid deep within her easily, her pussy a tight sheath around him. It felt so good that he groaned with pleasure as he jerked into her. His entire groin tightened as he thrust mercilessly, hinting that he wouldn't last long. It didn't matter how quick he was, knowing that she was his and that soon he could have her this way—and a hundred other, sinful ways—whenever he wanted fired his blood.

"Oh, oh, oh, oh!" Her cries of pleasure were delicious, each one more desperate, as if his thrust were bringing her to orgasm as fast as he was rushing there. "Oh! Oh! Fabian! Oh!"

"Alice!" Her pussy convulsed around him just as

pleasure exploded through him, from the base of his spine and out through his cock into her. He didn't usually come so hard, but something about Alice doubled every pleasure he'd ever felt before. His world narrowed down to the pleasure throbbing through him, then softened into a feeling of absolute bliss as he drew back and collapsed, spent, onto the bed.

The urge to sleep followed hard on the heels of his contentment. "Gorgeous," he managed to pant as he splayed against the sheets. "Perfect."

She flopped back to lay at his side. "I never knew that was possible."

He was tempted to laugh. More than tempted. The world seemed absolutely right and everything was as it should be. He should have taken Alice in his arms and kissed her tenderly, praising her for her bravery and sensuality. Instead, he fell fast asleep.

When he awoke an unknown amount of time later, she was gone. He shouldn't have been surprised. Alice had been clear that she had some sort of mission where his step-sister was concerned. But he felt her loss all the same. It pushed him out of bed and over to his washstand. The maid had been in at some point to relight the fire, and the day seemed well and truly started. He dressed as fast as he could, a smile on his face, then headed down-stairs to seek out his bride.

She wasn't at the table in the breakfast room, though at least a dozen of his mother's guests were. Everyone was chatting happily as the scent of cinnamon and tea filled the air. Fabian's stomach growled, but he walked out of the room moments after entering it. He wanted to find Alice, thank her again for the beautiful night and awakening, then lavish affection on her by feeding her sweets and waiting on her every need for the rest of the day. And that required that he find her.

He wandered the house until he heard her voice as he approached the library.

"...which is why it is of vital importance that you listen to me," she was in the middle of saying.

Fabian smiled. She must have found Georgette after all. He paused just outside of the library, pressing his back against the wall and giving her a final few moments to complete her business.

"I can assure you, my friend, you have nothing to worry about," Georgette said, a smile in her voice.

"Don't I?" Alice asked, clearly anxious. "Marriage is a trap that women cannot escape from."

Fabian's grin dropped and the muscles in his back and shoulders stiffened.

"My father's marriage machinations have proven to be nothing but disaster," she went on. "He has caused misery and ruin at every turn, and I would rather die than see you forced into an untenable position the way my sisters and I have been."

The tension gripping Fabian ratcheted up and he frowned. Was the thought of marriage to him truly that miserable to Alice?

"Truly, you have no need to worry on my behalf,"

Georgette went on. "I am flattered by your father's attentions, but I would never consider marriage to him."

"You must be on your guard, though," Alice rushed on. "It is not as easy as all that to avoid marriage, even when one does everything right. Believe me, I know."

"I do not doubt it," Georgette said cautiously.

"You must learn from the plights of me and my sisters. All three of us had husbands thrust on us against our will simply to feed our father's ambition and lust for money, though Imogen was fortunate enough to wiggle out of her sentence. Lettuce and I have not been so lucky."

Fabian's frown hardened into a scowl. Was that what Alice thought? That their forthcoming marriage was a prison? How she could still feel that way after moaning like a harlot for him as he took her from behind not more than three hours ago wasn't just a mystery, it was an insult. He wouldn't stand by and let himself be spoken of like that.

"Beware of spending too much time in my father's company or of being left alone with him," Alice went on.

Her words ended with a sharp gasp as Fabian stepped into the room, glowering and certain he looked like the devil come to snatch her.

"Fabian." Georgette stepped away from the fire, where she and Alice were talking, and crossed the room to greet him. Her sisterly smile dropped to concern as soon as she saw his expression. She glanced over her shoulder to Alice, a light of understanding glinted in her eyes, then she turned back to him. "I'll just leave the two of you alone," she said before rushing out of the room.

Fabian nodded as she hurried past him, then fixed his stare on Alice. His reluctant bride's face had gone pink and her eyes wide, but he couldn't tell whether her expression was fear or desire or alarm. Perhaps it was all three.

"So I am a trap set by your father, am I?" he asked, getting right to the point as he marched up to her.

"I—that is—oh." She wrung her hands in front of her, darting a glance toward the door as if she might bolt.

"You didn't seem to think marriage to me was such a prison sentence last night," he growled, hurt getting the better of him.

"It's not that," she said, clearly flustered. She bit her lip and glanced pleadingly up at him.

Part of Fabian wanted to be moved by the clear misery in her eyes, but too great a part of him felt as though that misery was an unbreakable wall that would always come between them. "If this is the way you feel about marriage to me, then why not call the whole thing off?"

"On—but I—"

"You have that within your power," he reminded her. "I cannot be the one to put an end to our engagement, but you can."

"That's not what I—"

"Why not, if the idea of being married to me is so odious? Why not call the whole thing off?"

54

"No one is calling anything off."

A burst of prickles, like icicles falling down his back, hit Fabian as Lord Stanhope stepped out from the doorway at the end of the room that led to one of the parlors. He glowered at Alice so hard that she jumped closer to Fabian's side, almost as if she would hide behind him.

"Lord Stanhope." Fabian greeted the man by clasping his hands behind his back and bowing a few, sharp inches. What was the man doing there? Had he over-heard the entire conversation? Had he been listening in on Alice's conversation with Georgette?

"No one is calling off any weddings," Lord Stanhope growled, marching up to Alice as if going to war. "Do you hear me?"

"Y-yes, Papa," Alice stammered, shrinking a few more steps toward Fabian. She glanced up at his deep frown, gulped, then inched way from him.

A maelstrom of emotions raged instantly to life in Fabian's gut. Alice was afraid of her father. That seemed to fit with what she'd been telling Georgette. Indeed, Lord Stanhope looked like the kind of man who terror-ized women as he marched up to Alice's side and grabbed her wrist.

"This marriage *will* take place," he hissed. "You will not wriggle out of it, like your useless sister did. I demand that you live up to your duties. Do you hear me?"

"Yes, Papa," Alice said, barely above a whisper.

"I'll thank you to unhand my bride," Fabian said in a

threatening voice. Within seconds, he'd gone from furious with Alice for what he saw as her dishonesty and deception to ready to protect her with his life.

Lord Stanhope let go of Alice and pivoted to face him, eyes narrowed. "Christmas is in four days," he said. "The wedding will take place on Christmas day. I won't have you backing out of this deal either. Everything has been arranged, and it will all continue as planned."

Fabian pulled himself to his full height, returning the man's threatening look with one of his own. To refer to the marriage of his daughter as a "deal" was despicable. But it also brought everything into shocking clarity. Lord Stanhope wanted to profit from marrying his daughter to a wealthy and famous man. He'd always known it, but now it seemed even more despicable.

"The wedding will take place," Fabian said, though not for the reasons Lord Stanhope wanted it to.

"Good." Lord Stanhope nodded, then promptly marched from the room without a backward glance for his daughter.

Alice's shoulders slumped and she sucked in a fast breath that might have been a prelude to a sob. She held herself together long enough to mumble, "If you will excuse me, my lord, I require breakfast."

She too fled from the room before Fabian could think of anything to say to stop her. He watched her go, staring at the empty doorway with a frown long after. Something was desperately wrong. The situation between Alice and her father was worse than he ever could have imagined.

He had the power to save Alice, he was sure, but at the moment, in spite of her amorous tendencies, there was a block between them that needed to be removed. And that block was clearly Lord Stanhope. The man had to be taken out.

CHAPTER 5

"It was uncanny and desperately wrong," Fabian told Matthew two days later, as the two of them enjoyed fortifying nips of brandy in one of the family's private, upstairs sitting rooms before heading down to the massive, Christmas ball.

Fabian's mother had invited what felt like half the county to the grand, festive event. The entire house had been in a state setting up for it during the last few days. So much so that Fabian hadn't had any time at all to address the odd scene he'd witnessed between Alice and her father in the library. He hadn't been able to get Alice alone to ask her about it either, and not for lack of trying. Every time an opportunity presented itself, Alice would rush away from him as though he were the very devil come to steal her soul.

Of course, it wasn't lost on him that he'd stolen something else that was precious to her. He'd lain awake the last two nights, hoping she would steal back into his room for more, rousing bedsport. His anticipation and longing for her was so acute that he'd resorted to sporting with himself, which he hadn't done since he was a green boy at university. But Alice had stayed away, at night and during the day.

"What could be wrong about a father instructing his daughter on her upcoming nuptials?" Matthew asked, swirling the dark liquid in his tumbler. He wasn't asking as if to dismiss Fabian's concerns, but rather like a scientist attempting to discover the root cause of a new phenomenon.

"He was cold," Fabian said. He swallowed the last of his brandy, set his glass on the table, then paced to the window. "Ice cold."

Outside, the world was a perfect winter landscape. Snow had fallen during the afternoon, blanketing everything in pristine white, but it wasn't enough to keep his mother's guests away. They were already arriving in a line of carriages that stretched to the edge of the property. Rows of lanterns lined the drive at equal intervals, each one decorated with greenery and ribbons. Fabian could just make out the edge of the decorations around the front door that welcomed guests to the ball in the style of the season.

Everything was festive and bright, but he couldn't shake the feeling that a deeper darkness lurked in the shadows.

"What I don't understand," he continued his

thoughts, turning back to Matthew and pacing in his direction, "is why Lord Stanhope was listening in on his daughter from the adjoining room."

"Are you certain he was listening and that it wasn't a mere coincidence that he appeared when he did?" Matthew asked.

Fabian rubbed his chin, then shook his head. "The timing was too precise. Not to mention that there is nothing in the room adjacent to the library but dusty artwork and ancient furniture."

"It's not often used," Matthew agreed. He finished his brandy then fell into pacing with Fabian, crossing paths with him in the center of the room.

"Aside from Lord Stanhope being where he shouldn't have been, what disturbed me about the incident was the fear in Alice's eyes," Fabian went on.

"She wouldn't be the first daughter who is afraid of her father," Matthew said with a tense frown.

Fabian knew too well what he meant. In his work designing gardens for England's wealthiest and most influential aristocrats, he'd been privy to far too many scenes of domestic misery. Some men used their position as the head of their household to terrorize and rule over the women in their lives. The practice was far too common, and it disgusted Fabian. After all he'd seen, he'd vowed that when he became a father, he would fill the lives of his wife and children with love, happiness, and enjoyment. He was far more inclined to follow the models of peasant families in Italy that he remembered from his own childhood, before Bonaparte's conquest had pushed his parents to flee to his mother's homeland until stability returned to the Italian States. The peasants might not have had money, but they'd had laughter, they'd had togetherness, and they'd had love.

"The other thing I don't understand," Fabian spoke again, starting back in the opposite direction and crossing paths with Matthew again, "is why Alice continues to run from me when I am the very person who could save her from her father's machinations."

To Fabian's surprise, Matthew laughed. "Friend, you realize that you *are* her father's machinations."

Fabian paused at the far end of the room, blinked, and turned to his friend. "Surely, she must see that I could be her savior."

Matthew shook his head, walking back to the center of the room. Fabian strode over to join him. "I overheard your Lady Alice talking to Georgette yesterday. She sees you as the bait in the trap her father set for her."

"I am not," Fabian balked.

Matthew shrugged, almost apologetically. "But you are. As much of a catch as the greater part of the host of mamas of England sees you to be, and as much as some young ladies swoon over you, with your exotic origins and devilish good looks, Lady Alice did not herself choose to become engaged to you."

Fabian frowned, still having a hard time accepting the possibility. "We got along quite well this summer, at Herrington's house party. We've gotten along exceptionally well since this party began." His face went hot at the admission.

Matthew answered the comment with a knowing grin. He and Fabian might not have been brothers by birth, but Matthew was like the sibling he'd never had, and Fabian had already told him everything about his night with Alice. All the same, Matthew said, "In my experience, it's all too easy for passion and trust to be entirely separate. You said she didn't end up in your bed deliberately—"

"But she didn't seem to mind being there once she was," Fabian cut his friend off before he could draw the same conclusion he'd been trying not to draw for days, that he'd done something underhanded and unforgivable. Even if it had seemed glorious at the time.

"Still," Matthew went on. "The facts are clear. Lady Alice might have enjoyed your activity the other night, but she is wary of you now. Her father is a bully who, it appears, has her under his thumb and has forced her into marriage with you."

"But we get along so well," Fabian argued, then sighed heavily. "At least, we did."

They both resumed pacing on opposite tracks, moving away from each other as they strode to the far corners of the room, then toward a spot where they crossed in the center of the room.

"Let's examine another fact," Matthew said after one turn about the room. "Lord Stanhope's other daughters were given away in marriage alliances as well."

"Except that the youngest eloped with Lord Thaddeus Herrington," Fabian added.

"But she would have been wedded to that disgusting, old brick, Sloane, if she hadn't," Matthew said.

"And the oldest was forced to marry Garland before being whisked off to America," Fabian finished the thought. He reached the end of the room, turned, and shrugged. "I am not half as disagreeable as either Sloane or Garland. At least, I hope not."

"You aren't," Matthew reassured him. "But in Lady Alice's eyes, you're the same as them."

"God, I hope not." Fabian sent his friend a wary look as they crossed.

Matthew only made it a few more steps before stopping and turning back to Fabian, his expression brightening. "But, you see, that is both the problem and the solution."

The mention of a solution caught Fabian's attention. He interrupted his pacing to stride up to Matthew's side. "I'm open to any solution that will end with Alice happily in my arms, as smiling as she was at the house party and as sinful as she was in my bed."

Matthew squared his shoulders as though he were a university lecturer about to give a speech. "Lady Alice has been distant because she is being forced to marry you. Her father is a tyrant, and she feels as though she is caught in his trap. It doesn't matter how sweet the bait is, she still feels as though she is being sent to the guillotine, not the altar."

"But what can I do about that? How can I make her see that I am her champion and, dare I say it, her savior?" Fabian asked, nearing the end of his rope.

"You can't." Matthew shrugged. "At least, not as long as she feels marriage to you is succumbing to her father's plots. However...." He arched one eyebrow, teasing Fabian with a grin.

"Don't toy with me, Matthew," Fabian growled.

Matthew laughed and shook his head. "The solution is simple, really. Lady Alice doesn't want you because her father does. But I believe, based on the evidence at hand, that if her father didn't want you, she would rush into your arms like a moth to a flame in an instant."

Fabian frowned, but Matthew's words had the ring of truth to them. "It can't be that simple."

And yet, a voice at the back of his head whispered that it could. Alice had been beyond biddable in his bed. She'd sighed and moaned with pleasure, taking more of him than he should have given. And in the morning, she had been as sweet as a ray of sunshine, admitting that she liked making love with him, even though he'd been a brute. There was absolutely enough between them to build a happy life with, if he could just take advantage of it.

He blinked out of his thoughts and focused on Matthew once more. "Are you suggesting that if Lord Stanhope suddenly believed me to be a bad match for his daughter, if he pressured her to call off and end things, Alice would do exactly the opposite and cling to me?"

"I believe so," Matthew said with a smile.

"So what do I need to do to convince the blackguard I'm a bad match?"

Matthew shrugged. "He pursued you for your fame and fortune, as well as your good name."

"I'm not eager to part with any of those things," Fabian admitted stiffly.

"You don't actually have to part with them," Matthew went on, the light of mischief in his eyes. "You only need to make Lord Stanhope think you've lost everything."

"And how do I do that?" Fabian asked, beginning to warm to the plan he could see his friend forming.

"Leave it to me," Matthew said, grinning. "All I ask is that you pretend we had more than a few brandies before the ball."

"Understood." Fabian nodded, his smile and his sense of heading into battle growing.

"And play along with whatever happens at the ball," Matthew finished. "Play along with everything."

THE LAST THING ALICE WANTED TO DO WAS ATTEND a ball. The last thing she wanted to do was be in Sussex at all. She sat by the window in her bedroom, delaying going downstairs to join the festivities, and thumbed through her well-worn pages of *The Secrets of Love*. She wished she and Imogen and Lettuce were together again, somewhere far away from their father and the misery he wrought on their lives. Of course, she would wish for Lord Thaddeus to be with them for Imogen's sake.

That thought brought another that left her squirming with heat and emotion. She wanted Fabian with them as well.

No, she didn't. Count Camoni was an instrument of her father's tyranny.

But he was magnificent. His body had felt heavenly against hers and inside of her. And he was kind, even if he'd gone along with her father's plans.

"It simply isn't fair," she wailed aloud, shoulders slumping.

She took comfort from the only thing that had lifted her spirits at all in the last few months. Well, the only thing aside from Fabian's wicked, wandering hands, his captivating mouth, and the hot thickness of his cock. She opened her segment of *The Secrets of Love* to where she'd left off and read.

"*Pleasure breeds contentment, and contentment gives rise to affection. Affection, in turn, demands more pleasure, causing increase in every measure. It is a mistake to think that love strikes us all, like a flash of lightning in a storm. For most, love is the gentle unfolding of pleasure, contentment, and affection in never-ending circles, like the petals of a rose overlapping and expanding as the rose blooms. Let yourself bloom as well. Let your petals unfurl slowly. Explore your lover over a lifetime, and do not be daunted if the bud between you seems closed at first.*"

Alice sighed and sank back in her chair, twisting to

glance out her frosty window into the night. The memory of the way Fabian had parted her legs and teased the petals of her womanhood rushed back on her, making her squirm in her seat. She wondered if that was precisely what the author of *The Secrets of Love* was talking about. It certainly felt as though she'd blossomed under Fabian's touch. And if she were honest with herself, she had more affection for him after the passion they had shared, in spite of not wanting to give in to him.

A frown creased her brow and she sat up, setting the ragged pages of her book aside. She couldn't submit quietly to her father's wishes. To do so would represent a failure of character on her own part, and it would be an insult to her sisters after the ordeals they had gone through. But Fabian was delicious. She'd come so close to begging him to hold her and take her to bed again in the last two days that she'd ended up forcing herself to stay away from him or be defeated.

Not that there was a single thing she could do to avoid marrying Fabian. She didn't have another man waiting to whisk her away, like Imogen had. She didn't even have a—

A rough knock sounded on her door before she could finish the thought, and a moment later her father burst into the room without waiting for Alice to bid him enter.

"What is the meaning of this?" her father demanded, shutting the door behind him and marching across the room.

Alice leapt to her feat, fear making her dizzy. "The

meaning of what, Father?" she asked, shifting away from her chair and attempting to keep her distance from him.

"You've poisoned Lady Georgette's mind against me, you little whore," her father growled.

"I...I didn't...." But, of course, she had.

Her father surged toward her, one hand raised. "Don't lie to me, bitch."

Alice squeezed her eyes shut, certain a blow would rain down on her. But nothing happened. She peeked at her father only to find him stepping back, flexing his hand.

"It would be noticed," he said, half to himself. "Questions would be asked. I won't have questions asked." He seemed to remember she was in the room. "I wanted Lady Georgette, and now I'm told my suit would be rejected if I should offer it. I blame you for this entirely."

Alice swallowed, trying not to cower under the force of her father's anger. She had finally made her case to Georgette and had been relieved beyond measure to find that Georgette wasn't in the lease bit interested in her father. In fact, a young viscount that she'd known since the two of them were children had made his intentions toward her clear just a few weeks before, and Georgette believed a Christmas proposal was imminent.

"I'm sorry," Alice whispered all the same, misery pressing down on her like a cloud of smoke.

"You should be," her father hissed. "And if you so much as dare to interfere with any future marriage alliances I might wish to make, I'll have your hide."

Alice gulped. Only when her father turned away from her and began pacing her bedroom did it dawn on her that in two days' time she would belong to Fabian and not him. How much could he hurt her if she were another man's wife?

He could hurt her by demanding he live with her and Fabian. He could hurt her by reminding her every day that she owed everything to his cleverness and his negotiations. He could tell her that without him, Fabian never would have looked twice at her.

She watched him as he strode to the fireplace and began fiddling with the various decorations arranged there. "There are bound to be eligible young women with fortunes at tonight's ball," he said, picking up a porcelain shepherdess, turning her over, and then setting her down again. He reached into his pocket with his left hand, drawing something out but concealing it. "You will not interfere if I make advances to them," he went on, picking up a small wooden box and opening the lid. "Do you understand?" he demanded, turning to face her.

"Y-yes, Papa." Alice wrung her hands in front of her, praying her father would leave. He was a tyrant in the best of times, but he had always made her ten times more nervous when he lingered in her bedchamber, as if he were contemplating the unthinkable.

He nodded with a grunt and faced the mantel once more, replacing the wooden box where it had been. "I want you to smile and be sweet and to request that your soon-to-be mother-in-law, the duchess, introduce me to the cream of her acquaintance tonight."

"I-I shall do what I can," Alice stammered.

"You will do as I say," her father bellowed, walking away from the fireplace to glare at her. "You will continue to do as I say even after your marriage. Count Camoni may be your stud, but I am your master and I always will be."

Tears stung at Alice's eyes but she nodded all the same. A horrible image of her father watching as Fabian mated with her the way they had in the morning, with her bent over as if in prayer while he lost himself in her, turned her stomach.

Her father took a step back, studying her with narrowed eyes. "Now. Get downstairs and join your fiancé. Dazzle his mother. Impress her friends. Recommend me to their daughters. Do you understand."

She nodded, but couldn't manage to say a word. She understood all too well. Not even marriage would free her from her father's grasp, and not even Fabian could save her.

CHAPTER 6

*A*lice's spirits were as low as could be as her father escorted her downstairs to the ballroom, or rather, dragged her. The last thing she wanted to do at the moment she felt the shackles close around her was to be seen in public, carousing and dancing, as her father demanded she do.

But almost from the moment she entered the ballroom, everything changed.

"Ah, Lord Stanhope. I see you have deliv—I see you have delelivered—I see you've devolverived—" Fabian slurred his words, unable to complete his sentence, and finished the whole thing with an indecorous burp. "You brought Alice."

A sound that was something between a gasp and a giggle caught in Alice's throat. She clapped a gloved hand to her mouth. Fabian was obviously in his cups.

"Count Camoni," her father growled, eyeing Fabian derisively. "Is something the matter?"

"The matter?" Fabian echoed in a voice higher and sharper than hers when she experienced a shock. "Oh, no, no, no, no, no, no—" He lowered his head as if executing a slow bow with each no, but stopped when he was nearly bent double, like an automaton that had run out of energy and needed to be wound up again.

Alice's eyes went wide as she watched him and made another choking, laughing sound. She never would have dreamed of seeing someone as elegant and noble as Fabian behaving like a child.

"Sir!" her father snapped. "Remember yourself."

Fabian snapped straight so fast that he nearly smacked a middle-aged couple crossing out to join the dance forming as they walked behind him. "I am Count Fabian Anthony Eduardo Camoni," he announced in a loud voice, drawing even more attention. Instantly, his shoulders sagged. "And I am ruined."

Alice dropped her hand from her mouth but continued to gape, sympathy and worry bubbling through her. "I'm so sorry to hear that, my lord," she said.

"What do you mean, ruined?" her father barked.

"I—" Fabian rubbed a hand over his face and sighed. "I cannot talk about it, sir. The pain is...." He paused, shaking his head, then whispered, "Too great."

Alice's insides fell into a jumble of conflicting emotion. It didn't matter how much of an instrument of her father's machinations Fabian was, he was clearly a man in distress. Distress that was the complete opposite of the command and sensuality he'd displayed with her the other night. As much as she hated it, he was her fiancé, and he was in trouble.

"Is there anything I can do?" she asked, taking a half step away from her father toward Fabian, brow lifted in cautious inquiry.

Fabian glanced to her...and Alice thought she caught a hint of mischief in his eyes. Her heart missed a beat. A moment later, Fabian took her arm and clung to her as though she were a lifeboat come to rescue him from a storm.

"Stay with me," he pleaded with her, his pathos so acute that it was unmanly. "Whatever happens next, you must stay with me."

"Of course," Alice answered before thinking about it.

"Has something happened?" her father asked, jaw tight, darting a glance around the room as more and more people craned their necks to see what was going on.

Fabian merely shook his head and made a show of reaching for Alice's hand. He fumbled it a few times, swaying slightly, before catching it and resting her hand in the crook of his arm. "There's naught to do at a time like this but weep and sing the songs of my people," he said before taking a deep breath and bursting into some sort of Italian peasant song at the top of his voice.

All around them, fussy older ladies and stiff gentlemen gasped and started. The ladies fanned themselves in alarm and the gentlemen huffed and quivered in outrage. Alice caught herself laughing before she could stop herself. Fabian had quite a good voice, in spite of the outrageousness of his song. He flung his free arm wide, knocking the old-fashioned wig on a pale-faced woman sideways. Alice laughed harder, smacking her free hand over her mouth.

"Stop your ridiculous behavior this instant," her father hissed, inching closer to Fabian but glaring around at anyone who dared to stare at them. "It is unbecoming for a man in your position."

"Ah," Fabian half said, half sang, his shoulders drooping again. "But you see, I am not a man in my position anymore."

"What?" her father's snapped question drew as much unwanted attention as Fabian's singing had.

Fabian drew in a breath. Just when Alice thought she would have an answer to his odd behavior, Lord Farnsworth rushed toward them, thumping a steadying hand on Fabian's back.

"You must excuse my step-brother, sir," Lord Farnsworth told Alice's father. "He's had a bit of a shock."

"Shock?" her father asked, suspicion pinching his face.

"Such a dreadful shock," Fabian sighed with theatrical intensity.

Alice narrowed her eyes in suspicion as well, but of a different sort than her father's. Theatrical. Fabian's eyes sparkled when he stole a glance at her. He was acting. Something was amiss, but she couldn't begin to imagine what would prompt him to put on such a performance in a room full of his mother's esteemed guests.

"I do not see how I will ever recover," he said with a sob in his voice. A false sob, Alice was sure.

"You are drawing untoward attention," her father growled through clenched teeth. "Pull yourself together, man."

"Yes, yes, I must do something," Fabian said, holding Alice's arm tighter and starting toward the side of the room. "I must do something soon."

Alice had the feeling he was about to do something shocking. She skipped along at his side all the same, feeling as though she were a carefree girl again, at play with friends.

"Count Camoni, I insist you cease this ridiculousness at once and tell me what has happened," her father demanded, following them to the side of the room. "I am to be your father-in-law in two days. It is my right to know what has befallen."

Lord Farnsworth came with them. It was he who answered, "Disaster, my lord."

Alice pressed her lips shut, watching Lord Farnsworth with wide eyes. He was obviously in on the joke as well.

"Spill it, man," her father hissed.

Lord Farnsworth took up a position on Fabian's other side, patting his back as though he were a disappointed child. "His Italian lands, sir," he said in a hushed voice. "They're gone."

"Gone?" her father boomed, recoiling as though Lord Farnsworth had announced Fabian had the plague.

"Gone," Fabian echoed morosely.

"Bonaparte," Lord Farnsworth whispered. He didn't elaborate. "And that's not all," he continued. "His reputation as a garden designer is in tatters."

"But—how can—one doesn't simply lose a reputation," her father sputtered.

"They do when the body of two of his workers are found planted along with the roses," Lord Farnsworth whispered. "Especially after a dispute about payment."

Alice gasped and pressed a hand to her chest. She tried to pull away from Fabian, but he held her tightly. When she glanced up at him in horror, however, his eyes continued to sparkle. He shook his head so slightly that she was almost convinced she'd imagined it.

They were definitely in the middle of a game, and she was determined to play along well.

"Oh, dear," she whispered. "No land and no reputation?"

"No," Fabian wailed, a hint of a grin tugging at the corners of his mouth. That grin turned into a full-fledged, if somewhat pathetic, smile as he turned and took both of her hands. "But at least I have you. Even if I have nothing else."

He leaned closer to her, and for a moment, Alice had the wild feeling that he was going to kiss her, right there, in a ballroom filled with distinguished guests, many of whom were watching. Even more shocking, she swayed toward him, tilting her head up, ready to be kissed. It was absolute madness, but her heart ached for him, in spite of how he fit into her father's plans.

"Just a minute," her father snapped. He grabbed Alice's arm and yanked her away from Fabian so hard that she nearly lost her balance. A flash of fury filled Fabian's dancing eyes, but her father went on. "The marriage isn't for two days. You don't have my daughter at all until then. Under the circumstances, I'm not sure if I approve of this match after all."

Indignation pulsed through Alice. Along with it, a burst of fear filled her. She'd already given herself to Fabian. For all she knew, his child could already be growing inside of her. And if he truly was in a desperate situation—which she wasn't entirely certain of—she couldn't abandon him because of it.

"Papa, you cannot mean to suggest that I should rethink my marriage to Count Camoni," she said softly, praying she was doing the right thing.

Fabian and Lord Farnsworth exchanged the barest of glances, a hint of triumph in both of their expressions. Something was certainly afoot.

"I'll not have you married to a reputed murderer and a pauper," her father growled. "In fact—"

"Lady Alice, would you care to dance?" Lord Farnsworth asked abruptly, bowing to Alice.

"I—" Alice's mouth fell open, but she wasn't

certain how to reply. She wanted to stay with Fabian and to find out what was truly going on. She wanted to protect him from her father, if she could. And if Fabian truly was playing some sort of game intended to thwart her father's machinations, she wanted to play a part.

"Go, my love," Fabian told her with a maudlin sense of drama. "I entrust you to Matthew's hands while I wallow in the depths of my misery."

He sent her a significant look. Alice peeked at Lord Farnsworth. He too seemed to be begging her with his eyes to trust the plan and do as Fabian said.

"All right," she said, hesitantly taking Lord Farnsworth's hand.

As Lord Farnsworth led her to the lines of couples forming for the next dance, her father growled, "What is the meaning of all this, Camoni? I demand you tell me all."

Alice wanted to know the truth herself. She had to wait until the dance began and she was able to steal a few, fleeting words from Lord Farnsworth as they made their way through the complicated steps.

"Your actions baffle me, my lord," she said as they crossed in the middle of the dancing rows.

When they came back together again for a turn, Lord Farnsworth said, "Trust us. We have a plan."

They were separated again as the dance took them in choreographed circles around other participants, but when they came back together for a promenade, Alice whispered, "Is this some sort of plan to thwart my father at his own games?"

"It is," Lord Farnsworth replied with a smile. "I can assure you, Fabian wants nothing to do with whatever evil plan your father is trying to force on you. He wants to help you."

"By losing all of his lands and his reputation?"

There wasn't time for an answer. The promenade ended, and Alice and Lord Farnsworth resumed a more intricate set of steps that kept them apart for too long to converse easily. Lord Farnsworth only had time to say, "You must trust us," and later, "All is well," as they turned and wove around each other.

The dance ended, but Alice's heart continued to beat up a storm in her chest. She curtsied to Lord Farnsworth with the final strains of the song, then allowed him to lead her back to where her father was still haranguing Fabian.

"This is not what I arranged," he was in the middle of saying. "I will not waste my daughter by tying her to a pauper and a rogue."

For one, fleeting second, Alice entertained the mad hope that her father's concern was for her and for her future happiness. She knew too well, however, that Lord James Marlowe, the Earl of Stanhope, only ever thought of one person—himself.

"I was counting on you," he continued, either not seeing Lord Farnsworth approach with Alice or not caring. "This match was to save my lands and to help prevent my title passing to my wretched brother."

"A man is nothing without his brother," Fabian said, straightening at the sight of Lord Farnsworth. "Or a loving wife."

He reached for Alice as Lord Farnsworth let her go, but before their hands could meet, Alice's father stepped between the two of them.

"I need a word with you," he growled, grabbing Alice's wrist and jerking her away from Fabian.

Alice yelped and glanced over her shoulder to Fabian as her father dragged her away. Every trace of silliness dropped from Fabian's expression, and he watched her as though he would ride in to rescue her if her father put one foot out of line.

"The engagement is off," her father growled as they came to a stop beside a potted plant.

Alice dragged her eyes away from Fabian and faced her father, eyes wide. "You ended it?"

"Not yet," her father said. "I have to speak to the duke and duchess." He stood a bit straighter, searching the room for Fabian's mother and step-father. "At least I'll have something to offer in your place."

"Whatever do you mean?" she asked, her stomach turning.

"I'll offer for Lady Georgette," he went on. "That's the only marriage that matters. I'll find another husband for you, someone with money who shares my sensibilities. I never should have entertained that fool Camoni's suit to begin with. Never trust a man who has a fancy for a woman."

"Count Camoni fancies me," Alice said, half to remind herself. She felt as though she were perched on the edge of a precipice, as though the rest of her life could be decided within minutes.

"What?" her father snapped, his expression pinching to sour fury.

For a moment, Alice thought she had spoken her thoughts aloud without being aware. A moment later, she saw what had prompted the single, bitter word from her father. Several yards ahead, Georgette had joined her father and Fabian's mother with a tall, handsome gentleman of distinction. They were both smiling as though the world had been served to them on a silver platter. The duke wore a broad smile as well and shook the gentleman's hand vigorously. The duchess hugged Georgette as though she were her own.

"Impossible," Alice's father grumbled. "I took no stock in the rumor. The whelp is barely a viscount. This is incomprehensible."

Alice swallowed, wondering whether she dared to tell what she knew. She settled on saying, "I had heard something to the effect of an engagement in the making for Lady Georgette."

"That was me," her father snapped. "That was supposed to be me. I made my intentions clear to her from the first. How dare the little bitch defy me?"

"I believe Lady Georgette has known and had feelings for Lord Loamley since they were children," Alice whispered.

Her father turned to her so fast and raised his hand so threateningly that, for a moment, Alice was certain he would strike her in public. He restrained himself, but not enough to avoid the notice of a cluster of middle-aged ladies standing near them. They all looked alarmed and began whispering as though deciding whether to come to Alice's rescue. One of them waved as if attempting to catch Fabian's eye. There was no need for the action. Fabian was already on his way over.

"This is not the end," Alice's father grumbled, tugging at the bottom of his jacket. "I have other plans in place. If I cannot restore my fortune one way, I shall restore it another."

"Lord Stanhope, is there a problem?" Fabian asked—sounding entirely sober and in control of his faculties—as he reached the potted plant where Alice and her father stood.

"No," her father answered, barely looking at Fabian. "There's no problem at all."

Without another glance at either Fabian or Alice, he marched off, weaving through several couples walking out to form new lines for the next dance and nearly upsetting a footman carrying a tray of empty punch glasses. He stormed through the ballroom door and out into the hall.

Alice let out a breath once he was gone, pressing a hand over her raging heart. "Thank heavens," she whispered, though the pressure only felt partially removed.

The air still sizzled, as though her father's machinations weren't done yet.

"Would you care to dance, my love?" Fabian asked with far more affection than Alice felt she deserved, but which she needed all the same.

"Nothing would give me greater pleasure," she said, taking Fabian's hand and walking with him to the center of the room.

Although judging by the spark in his eyes, quite a few things would give her more pleasure than merely dancing with him. She prayed she would get the chance to experience passion with him again and that her father's schemes didn't ruin everything.

CHAPTER 7

*D*ancing with Fabian was like walking out of a cramped and smoky house and into a pristine, spring garden, as far as Alice was concerned. It didn't even bother her that the steps of the dance frequently split them apart so that they were unable to carry on a conversation. With her father out of the room, Fabian had returned to normal. Judging by the way he executed the complicated steps of the dance with razor-sharp precision, he had no more been in his cups earlier than she had. The whole thing had been a ruse, and it was glorious to feel as though she was a part of it.

"Whatever possessed you to behave like such a buffoon earlier?" she asked all the same once the dance was over and Fabian escorted her to the side of the room.

Fabian glanced around, mischief sparkling in his eyes, before leaning closer to her and murmuring, "It was all part of a plot to save you, my dearest."

A strange, swooping sensation fluttered through Alice's stomach. She felt her cheeks go pink as she glanced up at him, not sure whether to smile or to feel like the lowest worm in one of his gardens. He watched her with absolute genuineness, affection that she didn't deserve radiating from him. She'd been such a ninny, shunning him as just another piece in her father's marriage games. And while a part of her thought she was justified in lumping Fabian into the same category as Lord Sloane or Mr. Garland, she felt as though her heart should have known better all along.

"Why would you want to save a silly miss like me?" she asked as they reached the side of the room, lowering her head.

"You're my fiancée," Fabian said.

She glanced up at him, shocked to find a look of surprise in his eyes. "I haven't given you any reason to like me," she said, her heart beating faster.

He let out a breath, bursting into a smile and resting his hand on the side of her face. "You've given me a great many reasons to like you."

"This summer, perhaps," she sighed, lowering her eyes even though he kept her from bowing her head. "I haven't behaved well since arriving at your mother's house."

"I've come to see why, though," he said in a more serious voice. He dropped his hand and shifted to stand beside her, his hands clasped behind his back. Alice wondered why until she saw a cluster of matronly, older women frowning at them in disapproval. "Your father is a villain," Fabian went on.

"He's my father," Alice sighed, assuming a respectable pose at his side. The old biddies tilted their noses up in grudging approval and went on with their conversation. Alice decided she truly hated being in the middle of a crowded ball when her heart and mind were at sixes and sevens. "One cannot choose one's father."

"No," Fabian agreed. "But one can marry and get away from him."

She peeked sideways at him, arching one eyebrow. "Do you truly think it will be that easy to escape from my father and his wheedling ways?"

Fabian dropped all pretense of pretend respectability and faced her fully again, taking her hands in his. "He can try to interfere all he wants, but I won't let him."

She sent him a weak smile. "I am grateful for the sentiment, but I doubt escape will be possible. You do not know the man like I do."

To her surprise, Fabian merely shrugged at her gloomy prediction. "If it comes to it, we will decamp from England and take up residence on my Italian lands. In fact, I would prefer if we did regardless."

Alice frowned in confusion. "I thought Bonaparte took away your Italian holdings."

An uncertain look pinched Fabian's face. "The Congress of Vienna restored Italian independence. The Habsburgs are nominally in control again, though I hear there is a strong movement for the unification of the peninsula afoot. The entire process has been chaotic, but my father's man of business has stayed near our land, even after my father's death, and I have hired him to sort through the bureaucracy of reclaiming the Camoni lands. I expect to hear from him at any time saying all is clear and it is safe to return home."

"Oh." Alice pressed one hand to her heart. Perhaps there was a means of escaping her father after all.

No sooner had hope filled her than heartache set in again.

"He wants to call off the wedding," she sighed, biting her lip and glancing out to the center of the ballroom, where Lord Farnsworth had joined the new dance with another female guest. "I know my father. I've observed the way he's watched you and me and the events of the evening. I am certain he thinks he can broker a marriage with Lord Farnsworth now, as he is now the highest ranked, eligible man at this party."

Fabian laughed. "Impossible."

Alice glanced back to him, her brow lifting. Fabian scanned the room, then took her hand and led her swiftly toward the exit and into the hall. A good number of party guests had left the noise and bustle of the ballroom to carry on conversations in the hallway or some of the parlors nearby. Fabian whisked Alice past all of them. A slight frown creased his brow at the sight of so many other people who had invaded his mother's house.

"There's nothing for it," he said at last, drawing her around the corner in the front hallway and up the main flight of stairs. "Some things need to be discussed in private."

"And my father could be anywhere," Alice added, looking around with extra intensity as they mounted the stairs.

"Matthew deliberately put himself forward as bait for your father," Fabian said as they reached the second floor and started down a hallway that Alice recognized with a gasp. Fabian was taking her to his bedroom. "It was all part of the plan," he went on as though nothing were at all untoward in him sneaking her to his most intimate space.

"What plan?" she asked, her body heating at the memory of what had happened the last time they were in his bedroom.

They reached his door, and Fabian pivoted to grin at her as he turned the handle. "The plan to convince you to marry me in spite of the match appearing to be a manipulation on your father's part."

Alice opened her mouth to reply, but no words came out. She could no more defend her previous stubbornness and the coldness with which she'd greeted Fabian upon arriving at Holly Manor than she could defy her father outright.

A moment later, as Fabian drew her into his bedroom and shut and locked the door behind her, she couldn't have come up with any words at all if she'd tried. The familiar scent of his personal space ignited memories within her that left her short of breath. The sight of the bed reminded her of how she'd been bent double as he mastered her from behind. The warm light of the crackling fire made her feel as though she needed to shed every stitch of clothing she wore to keep from burning up.

"Has it worked?" Fabian asked, his voice deep, an impish grin spreading across his face.

"Has what worked?" Alice gulped at the wolfish glint in his eyes.

"Have I convinced you that I am not part of your father's insidious plan?" He stepped flush with her, snaking one arm around her back to pull her close. "Have I convinced you to give yourself wholeheartedly to me?"

A shiver swept through Alice from her head to her toes, settling in her core. She rested her hands on his chest. Even through the layers of his formal attire, she could feel the pounding of his heart.

"Is this why you brought me here?" she asked, fiddling with the buttons of his jacket. "To ravish me so that I have no choice but to marry you."

He answered with a lopsided grin. "To be fair, I did that the other night."

"Yes, but that was a mistake," she said, her breath coming in tighter gasps, pressing her breasts against the scooping line of her bodice. "This has a far more deliberate feel to it."

He laughed low in his throat and drew his hands up to the tops of her short, puffed sleeves, then tugged them down to expose her shoulders. Her bodice was unforgivably tight, and though Alice had the feeling he might have intended to expose her breasts with one, forcible jerk, the result was to pin her arms to her sides and to make her feel all the more constricted.

"Yes," he said, lowering his mouth to the line of her neck and brushing his lips across the top of her right shoulder. "This is deliberate." He kissed her shoulder and nipped her tender flesh, even as his fingers stretched across her back, seeking out the ties holding her in her gown. "I plan to deliberately make love to you in such a scandalous way that your reputation would be forever ruined if so much as a hint of what we've done were to be made public."

"Oh, my," Alice whispered, closing her eyes and leaning her head back as he trailed kisses across the front of her chest.

He found and loosened the ties of her gown, then tugged the bodice lower. Her breasts popped free just as his kisses rained over their tops. His mouth closed firmly around her right nipple. She sighed and made a wicked sound of pleasure as he teased it into a pert point.

"You really do have the most extraordinary breasts," he purred.

"They're too big," she gasped, her legs going wobbly as he brought one hand around to knead a breast and lave his tongue over its nipple.

"I like them big," he said, glancing up at her with a predatory grin. "There are so many things you can do with a pair of sizable tits."

His use of vulgar language triggered something delicious inside of her. She wriggled and shifted, doing what little she could to climb out of her restrictive clothing. "Such as?" she asked, breathless.

He seemed to sense what she wanted. He stepped back, walking behind her to undo the rest of the fastenings of her gown, then in front of her to push the whole thing down over her hips. It pooled on the floor around her feet as he went to work on the closures of her stays. Alice had been dressed and undressed by maids countless times in her life, but there was something deliciously erotic about being stripped by a man with such sensuality in his eyes. A fully clothed man at that. Fabian seemed in no hurry to remove his own clothes as he peeled away her layers, leaving her bare.

A needy shiver swirled up in her as he pulled away her stays and chemise, then undid her drawers and pushed them and her stockings down over her legs. "There," he said when she was fully naked. "If anyone were to come through my bedroom door and see you like this, the scandal would be so great that you would be forced to marry me, no matter your father's wishes."

"But your door is locked," she reminded him, every part of her fluttering. She didn't know what to do with her hands. The wild idea that she should touch herself while he watched filled her, but she was too overcome with the desire to see him undress to do it.

Fabian glanced over his shoulder at the door, then back at her, one eyebrow raised. "So it is. Anything can happen to a woman when she is in a man's bedroom with the door locked."

"Anything?" she echoed, her voice high and thready.

"She might find herself savaged by a man with uncontrollable lusts." He took a step toward her.

Alice backed up as he stalked her, until her legs hit the side of his bed. "Oh, my."

"Do you want to be savaged, Alice?" he asked in a voice as dark and velvet as the night sky.

Alice swallowed, her throat going dry. The way he looked at her body, as if he wanted to devour her as thoroughly as he had the night before, left her knees too weak for her to stand much longer. All she could do was nod and blush.

"It's difficult to be savaged by a man still dressed for a ball," he said.

It was all the command he needed to give. Alice reached for him, working open the buttons of his jacket with shaking hands. A hint of a grin played across Fabian's otherwise serious lips as she peeled his jacket back and started on the buttons of his waistcoat. He shrugged out of the jacket and tossed it aside, then disposed of the waistcoat as well as her hands dropped to the falls of his breeches.

His quick intake of breath was all the hint she had that he was pleased with what she was doing. His face remained an implacable mask of seriousness, although his eyes danced with mirth. There was something fun and erotic in the roles they'd fallen into so quickly. She was his submissive slave, helpless against whatever wicked things he wanted to do to her, and he was her master. The game made her bold and free to explore.

"What do you want from me, master?" she asked, blinking up at him as innocently as she could.

The flash of fire in Fabian's eyes was a clear sign that he wanted to play as much as she did. "I want you to pleasure me," he growled.

"Anything for you," she said.

She finished with the fastenings of his breeches, pulled the hem of his shirt up, and slid her hands against his cock as it sprung free. He growled deep in his throat, biting his lip.

"More," he demanded. "I want you on your knees."

Every hint of naughty things women could do to men that Felicity and Eliza and the other young ladies at the Herrington's house party had whispered about swirled back through Alice. She could barely catch her breath as she lowered herself to her knees, her head at the level of Fabian's hips.

He peeled his shirt off and tossed it aside, then said, "Remove my boots."

It wasn't what Alice had expected but she did as she was commanded anyhow. Their game was nearly upended as his boots gave her a devil of a time coming off. There was nothing at all sensual about yanking and tugging while he was forced to step back and lean against the bedpost for balance. Alice caught herself laughing at one point, but that laughter died in her throat when his second boot came off, leaving her staring at his erection as it poked above the sagging front of his breeches.

"Remove my breeches," Fabian ordered, leaning heavily against the bedpost and resting his arms behind his head.

"Yes, my lord," Alice said, scooting closer and grasping the garment.

She tugged them down slowly, her senses running riot as she revealed his hips, his thighs, and the alluring sack that was pulled tight beneath his impossibly thick and hard penis. She licked her lips as she studied that part of him, pushing his breeches and stockings down until he was able to step out of them.

That left him fully naked in front of her. He stood with his feet slightly apart, watching her with heavy-lidded eyes.

"I want you to swallow my cock," he said in a voice that resonated with desire and command. "As deep as you can. I want to see your lips tight around the base and hear you moan with pleasure as you sheath me."

"Yes, my lord," she managed in a shaky voice, aching with sinful desire.

She reached for him, caressing his sack and stroking his length. Prickles of desire broke out across her skin and her sex ached so desperately that she could feel it weeping. That only encouraged her to lean forward, bringing her mouth to the tip of his cock to tease and test it with a kiss.

The salty taste of him set her heart beating faster. He

was hot and hard in her hand, and curiosity raged within her. She knew what he felt like stretching her cunny, but she wanted to know what he would feel like in her mouth. She opened her mouth over his tip, tasting more of him and running her tongue across his slit. He sucked in a breath and groaned, tension rippling off of him.

He liked it. He liked what she was doing. That knowledge encouraged her. It filled her with power as she took a breath and drew more of him into her mouth. It was a strange sensation, like taking a bite of a delicious treat that was just a bit too much for her. Her tongue slipped along the underside of his cock as she slowly bore down on him, taking in as much of him as she could. He let out a wordless sound of delicious frustration and shifted his hips forward.

A moment of panic hit her as he went too far, nearly choking her. That panic quickly faded as she pulled back and took him in again on her own terms. She took her cues from him, sliding him in and out of her mouth, slowly at first, but with increasing speed and depth as he responded. She peeked up, excited by the look of abandonment on his face as she swallowed him. The look left her feeling paradoxically in control, and she gripped his thighs and made a long, low sound of pleasure.

"You'd be ruined if anyone saw you with my cock down your throat," he growled. "So you'll have to marry me now."

"I never want to marry anyone else," she said, taking a moment to breathe. "You're the only man I'll ever want."

She drew him into her mouth again, teasing him with her tongue for a moment before steeling her nerve and taking in as much of him as she could. She let him fill her, moving on him with sureness of purpose until she could feel his body tense, near release.

"Dear God," he gasped at last, pushing at her shoulders so that she rocked away from him. His cock sprung free, standing straight up between them. "Not like this," he growled.

She opened her mouth to ask what he wanted, but no sound came out before he scooped her under her shoulders and lifted her to her feet. He practically threw her onto the bed, then grabbed her knees and wrenched them apart. He wore a look of absolute concentration that bordered on desperation as he spread her. With another, swift, strong movement, he pulled her hips right to the edge of the bed then plunged into her.

The surprise of being impaled without warning only added to the deep, thundering pleasure as he moved inside of her. He braced himself on the bed and thrust into her hard and fast. There was no doubt at all that he was claiming her as fiercely as any warrior had ever claimed a woman as his own, and within seconds, Alice teetered on the edge of ecstasy. She was wicked to love the way he used her, without mercy but with so much pleasure. A proper young lady would blush and weep at the brutish way he took her. But it felt so good that she throbbed into orgasm in short order, not caring if she was a shameless wanton for loving the way he mastered her.

Moments later, Fabian cried out as he spilled himself inside of her. His thrusts slowed, but the intensity of sensuality and the heat between them barely lessened. He climbed fully onto the bed with her, shifting her into his arms and entwining their sweating bodies in a knot that no one, not even her father, could untangle.

"Never doubt that I want you," he panted, brushing his hands over her sides and breasts as though they were just getting started instead of finishing. "You've endeared yourself to me in so many ways, including this one."

"I meant it when I said I never want to be with another man for the rest of my life," she said, as breathless as he was. "You can do anything you want to me, use me in any way you see fit. I love it and I—" She hesitated, uncertain whether she wanted to lay herself completely bare. A heartbeat later, she knew she did. "I love you," she said.

He tensed for a moment before relaxing, like a flag unfurling. "Darling," he said, rolling her to her back and cradling her breast. "I love you too."

Alice smiled, feeling safe and at peace for the first time in so long she couldn't remember. Everything would work out the way it should after all.

"Now," Fabian continued, mischief back in his eyes. "Let's see how many times I can make you come before we're too exhausted to move."

CHAPTER 8

For the second time within a week, Fabian awoke with Alice nestled in his arms. He grinned and shifted to cradle her body more fully with his, deep contentment infusing him. The first, cold rays of December light, the dawning of Christmas Eve day, peeked through the gaps in the heavy curtains covering his windows. The fire in the grate crackled merrily, hinting that the maid had crept in to light the fire earlier. The bed was toasty and comfortable, and Fabian counted himself the luckiest man in the world.

He nuzzled against Alice's hair, which had been taken down after their first round of love-making and now rested in soft waves across the pillow and her shoulders. He stroked a hand along her side, loving the soft warmth of her curves. She smelled of heaven itself—the fading scent of perfume, the salt of her skin, and a hint of musk leftover from their night together. She'd been mind-bogglingly experimental and free with her sexuality. He'd gotten carried away and was more demanding of her than he should have been, but Alice had seemed to enjoy their bedsport as much as he had.

A man could do much worse for himself when it came to marrying. One more day and he and Alice would be joined forever in the sight of God and man.

He had just circled his hand around to her belly and was debating starting the morning by stroking her into orgasm when an urgent knock sounded on his door.

"Fabian." Matthew's voice was as serious as the grave. "Wake up and look lively."

A deep frown creased Fabian's brow and he was tempted to shout all sorts of profanities at his friend, but sense took over. Matthew wouldn't interrupt a perfect morning unless something had happened.

"What's going on?" Alice asked, coming awake slowly. She twisted to her back and slowly pushed herself to sit, rubbing her eyes. She made no effort to keep the bedcovers from sliding down to her waist, exposing her glorious breasts.

Fabian sat as well, fighting to resist the urge to ogle her beautiful form or to forget about whatever Matthew was trying to warn him of to make love to her again. "Something must have happened," he said instead, scooting to the edge of the bed and standing.

Alice made a giggling sound of delight, and when

Fabian glanced back at her, she was grinning at him and looking like the perfect picture of a debauched woman. Her hair was disheveled, her skin flush with desire, and her eyes sleepy with satiety and a hint of eagerness for more. Fabian couldn't help but turn abruptly and walk back to the bed.

He leaned over to kiss her soundly, grabbing the headboard and pressing her back against it. "I wish there were time for me to thoroughly ravish you again," he said, his body urging him on and his cock stiffening. "As of tomorrow, I won't let anything or anyone keep me from burying myself deep within you as often as I'd like."

Alice hummed low in her throat, circling her arms around his neck. "I'll be yours to command," she said. "Patience truly does have its rewards."

He kissed her one final time, then pulled away and set to work washing and dressing as fast as possible. Alice dragged herself out of bed and made an attempt to tidy herself and dress as well. They made only minimal progress before another knock sounded at the door.

"Fabian, you're needed at once." This time it was Georgette's voice that drifted conspiratorially through the door. "And Alice, if you're in there, hurry back to your room with all haste. It...it may already be too late."

Fabian's brow shot up at the direness in Georgette's warning. He exchanged a glance with Alice, who had gone slightly pale. There was less shock in her expression than there was dread, as if she knew what kind of horror awaited them.

They checked themselves one final time to be certain they were presentable, then Fabian crossed to the door and peeked into the hall.

"It's clear," he said, gesturing for Alice to come forward.

She skipped over to him and took his hand, and they proceeded into the hall. It would likely be as damning for them to be seen together so early in the morning, slipping quietly through the upstairs halls, as it would have been for anyone to walk in on them in the throes of passion the night before, but Fabian no longer cared. Alice would be his wife in just over twenty-four hours, and she needed his protection. There was no doubt in his mind that whatever was afoot in the house, her father had something to do with it.

As it turned out, he was right, but not in a way he expected.

"Thieves," his mother said, fury in her eyes, as he and Alice joined the rest of the family in the breakfast room. "Our house has been infiltrated with thieves."

Prickles raced down Fabian's back as he let go of Alice's hand to cross to his mother and greet her with a kiss to her cheek. Out of the corner of his eye, he saw Lord Stanhope move from the spot where he'd been standing at the side of the room—a spot that seemed designed to allow him to be unobtrusive while observing everything—and over to Alice's side. Fabian wanted to rush to Alice and defend her against whatever evil her father was planning, but his mother had already gripped his arm with worried desperation and was looking at him for help.

"What has been stolen?" he asked, shifting so that he could address his mother and still keep a full eye on Alice.

"All manner of things," his mother said. "Jewels that were removed from our guests throughout the night, valuable objects throughout the house, and even a purse that was taken from Lord Aylesbury's room."

"The items are small," the duke added, coming to stand by Fabian's mother's side, "but taken together, they are of considerable value."

"It chills me to the bone to think that we have somehow allowed a thief into our midst," his mother said, letting go of Fabian and clinging to her husband's arm instead. "Who could have done such a thing?"

Fabian was certain he knew exactly who could do it. But when he turned a sharp glare to Lord Stanhope, he found the bastard clutching Alice's arm, hissing something in her ear. Alice had gone white and leaned away from her father, but it was clear he wouldn't let her go anywhere.

ALICE'S HEART FELT AS HEAVY AS A STONE AS IT SANK into her stomach. She never should have left Fabian's side. She should have followed him when he approached his mother. Now, with her father's hands clamped around her arm, she felt well and truly trapped.

"I will not let that bitch, Lady Georgette, humiliate me this way," her father growled into her ear. "She had a fiancé waiting for her all along. The engagement was announced late in the ball last night." He paused. "I noticed you were absent."

"I...I'd gone to bed," Alice whispered, peeking sideways to where Fabian was talking with his mother and the duke.

"Yes, you had," her father said, lasciviousness thick in his tone. The way he looked at her made Alice's skin crawl. "Fortunately, your whoring will help me in the long run."

"I...it will?" She gulped. Anything that her father thought would help him was not good for her.

"I'd thought to wed you to Lord Farnsworth," her father went on, bitterness lacing his voice. "But when I approached him about the match, he put me off. Said his intentions lay elsewhere."

A strange and paradoxical feeling of relief washed through Alice, but only for a moment. Her father looked too pleased for that to be all there was.

"Fortunately, I have been working on another means of securing a fortune," he said. "And as soon as you are free from your obligations toward Count Camoni, I can look for a higher bidder to marry you off to."

"But Fabian and I are to marry tomorrow," Alice said, her voice and her heart failing her.

"I plan to take care of that," her father growled.

Fabian turned to check on her at just that moment.

He stepped away from his mother and the duke and marched toward her with the look of an avenging angel.

A spring of hope welled up within Alice, but it was squashed when her father said, "I have your thief right here." He gripped her wrist hard and dragged her toward the duke and duchess.

Dread swirled in Alice's stomach, and she thought she might be sick. "I didn't steal anything," she tried to defend herself in a small, pitiful voice.

"The thief is my wicked daughter," her father charged on. "She is a thief and a whore."

"I'll thank you not to insult my fiancée," Fabian growled, moving until he stood toe-to-toe with Alice's father, towering over him with his full, intimidating height.

"I doubt you'll want her after what I can tell you," her father went on, a sly grin stretching across his wicked face. "Even though you've already had her."

A few of the guests who sat around the breakfast table but hadn't, until then, been a part of the conversation gasped and stared at Alice with wide eyes. The duke scowled and the duchess looked thoroughly scandalized. She marched up to Fabian's side, indignation in her eyes, and asked, "What is the meaning of this?"

"I can explain, Mother," Fabian said.

"My daughter is your thief, and she has thrown herself at your son in the basest possible ways," Alice's father blurted before Fabian could go on.

"Fabian, is this true?" the duchess asked.

A flush painted Fabian's face and he appeared to be at a loss for words. "Alice is not a thief," he said at last.

"She is a deceiving whore who has fooled you all," her father went on, staring particularly at Fabian. "I only regret that I introduced her into your life. I should have known that she could not be reformed."

"Alice is a good and sweet woman," Fabian argued, turning to his mother. "Her father has used and abused her and her sisters for years now. He married, or at least attempted to marry, her sisters for his own financial aim. He targeted me as someone who could enrich him, and the moment he thought I was no longer solvent, he tried to involve Matthew in his schemes."

"It's true," Lord Farnsworth said, stepping forward.

"I would never dream of importuning such a lofty and noble family in such a way," Alice's father insisted, looking genuinely offended. "I hold your entire family in highest esteem."

"You have sought to scheme and cheat us at every turn," Fabian insisted.

His mother and the duke appeared completely flummoxed, glancing from Fabian to Alice's father in turn as each one spoke, as if they didn't know who to believe.

"If you think I am being anything but earnest with you," Alice's father went on, "then search my daughter's room. Turn it upside down and go through all of her things. I think you'll find exactly the proof you need there."

The duke glanced to one of the footmen that hovered

near the door, eyes wide. The young man turned and dashed from the room.

"And as for my daughter's low moral character," her father went on with a sniff, looking Alice up and down with a sneer. "You will notice she is still dressed in the same gown she wore to the ball and her appearance is damning."

Alice glanced down at herself, her heart sinking lower than it had already gone. She looked a fright. Anyone with eyes and a brain could see she'd spent the night in Fabian's arms.

"Investigate Count Camoni's bedchamber if you don't believe me," her father went on.

"There is no need to investigate anything," Fabian cut in with a booming voice before her father could add anything else. He turned to his mother with an apologetic look. "It is true, Mama. Lady Alice and I have anticipated our vows. But seeing as our wedding is to take place tomorrow morning—"

"I would be shocked if you considered going ahead with plans to see your son and my daughter married," Alice's father interrupted. "I cannot believe that someone of your rank and visibility would consent to have a thief and a whore in your family."

Again, the guests whose breakfast had turned into the circus they were witnessing gasped and stared at Alice. She had never felt so humiliated in her life.

"My son and his betrothed would not be the first

couple to anticipate their vows," the duchess began slowly.

"You would connect your family with a thief?" Alice's father feigned utter horror at the idea. And the emotion was feigned. Alice had known her father too long to doubt his playacting. There was too much of a glimmer of triumph in his eyes, too much glee that he was the center of attention and he was getting his way.

"Alice is not a thief," Fabian insisted. "And I will not abandon her when she needs me the most, particularly if that means this monster will continue to hold sway over her."

"Oh, dear," the duchess said, studying Alice, then Fabian, then looking to her husband for help. "I don't know what to do. I suppose—"

"We found it, my lady." The footman who had darted out of the room such a short time ago returned, holding up what appeared to be a priceless brooch. He skittered to a stop just inside the breakfast room, eyes bright, but seeming to remember his place. He quickly stood at attention.

"What have you found?" the duke asked, approaching him.

"This brooch, my lord." The footman handed over the brooch. "It was in a box on the mantel. Mr. Davies has the rest of the staff turning Lady Alice's room inside out to find more."

"You see?" Alice's father asked with a look of triumph. "I told you she was a thief."

The duchess looked genuinely distressed. The duke turned to glower at Alice. Fabian appeared equally furious, but his glare was for Alice's father.

Alice sagged in defeat. "You put that there," she told her father, knowing it wouldn't do a lick of good. "I saw you put something in that box on my mantel the other day. You're laying blame at my feet on purpose." Her words weren't an accusation. She was too exhausted, too defeated to accuse him of anything. All hope left her. There was no way she would escape his clutches now. The duchess had proof that she was everything her father had accused her of being.

"This is impossible," Fabian said, coming to her defense all the same. "I believe Alice when she says her father planted the brooch in her room."

"You think I'm the thief?" Alice's father demanded, his face going red.

"No one accused you, Lord Stanhope," Lord Farnsworth said. "But if you are accusing yourself...."

"I am no such thing," Alice's father snapped. "Search my rooms. Search all of my things. You will find nothing that does not belong to me."

"Surely, you have hidden it all somewhere else," Fabian growled.

"How dare you accost me so?" Her father continued to act out his innocence to a ridiculous degree. "I should take my daughter and leave this house at once."

"No," Alice yelped, leaping toward Fabian. He caught her with one arm and held her close.

"Enough of this," the duke boomed, silencing everyone. He glanced to his wife.

The duchess chewed her lip, studying Alice and her father, Fabian, the footman, and even Lord Farnsworth. "I don't know what to believe," she said at last. "Lady Alice has always seemed pleasant and affable to me. But if she has been with my son...." She pressed her lips shut and shook her head. "I cannot make any decision now. More evidence needs to be collected."

"More?" Alice's father demanded, as if all his efforts to lay a trap hadn't been enough.

The duchess glanced to him with a frown, then to Fabian and Alice. "I will give you until the end of the day to disprove the accusations of theft made against Lady Alice, and to find the true thief, if possible. But if you cannot come up with an explanation for stolen items being found in her room—"

"Lord Stanhope planted the brooch there, you heard Alice," Fabian growled.

"—then I will have no choice but to insist the engagement be called off," his mother continued, holding up her hands. She sent her son a sympathetic look. "I am thinking of you and you alone, my dear. If this truly is some sort of ploy to embarrass all of us, then I cannot allow it."

"And if it is merely a concoction of Lord Stanhope's to take Alice back so that he can sell her in marriage to someone willing to pay a higher price?" Fabian asked.

His mother looked genuinely sympathetic as she said,

"Then I pray you find the proof you need before the end of the day."

CHAPTER 9

*N*othing was going to prevent Fabian from marrying Alice. Not her father and not even his mother.

"I'll find all the proof you need, Mama," he said, fixing his mother with the same stubborn look he'd given her as a boy when he wanted to get his way, then glaring at Lord Stanhope. "I will prove to you that Lady Alice is an angel who has been held in the clutches of a devil for too long."

"How dare you?" Lord Stanhope growled, seemingly indignant. There was a flash of fear in his eyes, though, as if he hadn't expected to encounter a foe as determined as Fabian. Or—which only enraged Fabian more—as if he didn't believe his daughter was worthy of having a champion.

Fabian didn't answer Lord Stanhope's feigned indignation. He crossed to Alice, taking her hand in his and leading her out of the room before anyone could stop him.

"Would you like to bathe and change into something fresh before we begin this hunt?" he asked her in a soft voice as he whisked her into the hall.

"Oh, yes please," Alice answered in a tiny voice that was both relieved and distraught.

"We'll go to your room first, then."

They had only made it a few yards down the hall when Lord Stanhope burst out of the breakfast room and chased them, shouting, "Just where do you think you're going with my daughter?"

"She is my fiancée," Fabian insisted, pivoting to glare at the man as they reached the front hallway.

Lord Stanhope reeled back as if Fabian had struck him. A moment later, he recovered himself enough to say, "Not for long. She'll be found guilty of theft and cast out by your mother and all good society." He rubbed his hands together, grinning at his daughter with glee. "I know of a sugar merchant who has been looking for a titled bride. He's worth a fortune, and with the information I have about the way he cheats his business partners and starves his slaves, I'll make a fortune off of him in blackmail."

Disgust turned Fabian's stomach. He inched closer to Alice, sliding a protective arm around her waist. "The moment I prove that you are the thief, you will never see or have anything to do with Alice again."

He turned and marched on, drawing Alice with him.

Lord Stanhope sputtered and snorted, then caught up with them again on the stairs.

"You won't be able to prove anything," he said, a light of cunning in his eyes.

That was all the confession Fabian needed. Lord Stanhope was certainly guilty of theft and more. He just had to prove it.

"You know the way your father's mind works," he told Alice when they reached her room.

A harried-looking maid was already at work, taking Alice's things out of the wardrobe as though she'd been ordered to pack.

"Help Lady Alice to wash and dress, please," he ordered the maid.

"But her father said they were leaving this morning," the anxious maid said, sending a look that was almost guilty in Alice's direction. "He said I was to pack."

Fabian shook his head. "She's not going anywhere. Help her to wash and dress."

The maid chewed her lip and curtsied, then rushed to Alice to help her out of her wrinkled ball gown. She sent a wary look Fabian's way. He assumed she felt awkward about undressing Alice with him in the room, but he wasn't about to leave Alice alone. Not for one second. He turned his back to spare the maid's feelings.

"You believe that I'm not the thief?" Alice asked as she undressed.

"You would never do anything so base," Fabian said, crossing his arms and staring at a painting of dryads frolicking in the woods. He would have done anything to see the sort of happy, carefree, lustful expression on Alice's face as those dryads wore.

"I cannot tell you what that means to me," Alice said with a sad sigh of relief.

Fabian heard her move to the washstand at the far end of the room. The sound of water splashing into the basin followed. He caught sight of the maid moving to the bed to select fresh clothes out of the corner of his eye.

"My father put that brooch in the box on my mantel," Alice went on. "I saw him do it just before the ball yesterday, though I didn't know what I was seeing at the time."

"I believe you," Fabian said with a nod.

He spotted a curious stack of papers on her bedside table and strode over to pick it up. It turned out to be a section torn from a book. The typeface was frilly and delicate, and the title of the chapter on the top page, *The Delicate Flowering of Love*, made him grin.

"What's this?" he asked, picking up the book.

"Oh!" Alice gasped and sped across the room to take the partial book from his hands. "That's...it's...."

Fabian twisted to grin at her. Her cheeks were bright pink, as were the tops of her breasts and the curve of her backside. She'd rushed to his side without dressing and without drying. A sheen of rose-scented water covered her luscious body. Fabian forgot what he'd asked her, forgot their mission, forgot everything but the need that slammed through him, making his breeches uncomfortably tight.

It was only the shocked squeak of the maid that kept him from tossing Alice over her bed and fucking her silly. He cleared his throat and settled for kissing her tenderly instead.

"You'll have to read aloud to me from this book later," he said in a low voice, suspecting what kind of information it contained. "For now, we must focus on proving your innocence and your father's guilt."

"Thank you," Alice said, glancing up at him with wide eyes filled with affection. "You cannot imagine what it means to me for you to stand by my side this way."

He couldn't resist kissing her again, though he didn't dare risk putting his arms around her. Maid or no maid, he wouldn't be able to stop himself if he touched Alice too much.

"Finish dressing," he said with a smile. "And then we'll begin our hunt by searching your father's room."

Alice handed the partial book back to him then skipped back to the maid, who held her underthings and watched them with a look of sentimentality. As Alice dressed, Fabian flipped through the pages of her book. His brow shot up more than once at vivid illustrations and lurid descriptions of acts of love. A grin spread across his face and he promised himself they would attempt each and every act described on the pages.

There would be time for passion and play later. As soon as Alice was dressed and presentable, he took her hand and led her out into the hall once more.

But as they reached the hall where Lord Stanhope's room stood, they were blocked.

"I refuse to allow you into my private chambers," the bastard himself said, standing in the doorway.

Fabian pulled himself to his full height, towering over him. "You refuse me entrance into a room in my mother's house?"

"Yes," Lord Stanhope said. "And furthermore, I find it insulting that you would even attempt to infiltrate the sacred space of a guest in the duke's house."

Fabian clenched his fist and opened his mouth to argue, but a small tug on his sleeve stopped him. He turned to find Alice glancing up at him, urgency and inspiration in her eyes. Without another word for Lord Stanhope, he rested his hand on Alice's back and walked several paces down the hall with her.

"He's bluffing," she whispered when they were far enough away not to be overheard. "He wants you to believe he's hiding something in his room so you waste time getting past him and checking."

"Do you think so?" Fabian asked.

Alice nodded, peeking past him to where Lord Stanhope was watching the two of them with narrowed eyes. "It is likely that he has someone else working for him, someone who is busy at this very moment, hiding what he's stolen."

Fabian clenched his jaw, frustrated that he had to stoop so low as to deal with someone so cunning. "Where would he hide his loot if not in his own room?" he asked.

Alice bit her lip and glanced at her father once more before walking away, gesturing for Fabian to come with her. "Have you noticed that he has appeared in strange places, places he wasn't expected to be, these last few days?"

"I have noticed," Fabian said. He took Alice's hand and picked up his pace. "We should start by searching the ballroom. He's devilish enough to have hidden what he stole in plain sight."

Alice nodded, and the two of them rushed downstairs to the ballroom. The servants were still hard at work, cleaning up after the night's festivities. It usually took a full day for the ballroom to be set back to normal—or in this case, normal decorated with Christmas greenery, bows, bells, and other festive bits of the season—which would have given Lord Stanhope and any accomplices plenty of time to retrieve hidden loot.

But as hard and as long as Fabian and Alice searched, they came up empty-handed.

"It's not here," Alice said with a disappointed sigh.

Fabian hated the worry and defeat in her expression. "The library," he said. "Your father appeared in the library without warning the morning you attempted to speak to Georgette."

"You're right." Hope returned to Alice's eyes.

They headed out of the ballroom and through the hall to the library at the other end of the house.

"He could have concealed anything behind the books," Fabian said, marching toward the shelves at the far end of the room, near the door Lord Stanhope had appeared through. He took a moment to glance into the next room, but the parlor on the other side was dusty and unused. Still, the thought it would be wise to search that room as well.

"He may not have hidden everything together," Alice said, pulling books from shelves and feeling behind them. She yelped almost immediately and withdrew her cobweb-covered hand. "I'm not so certain I want to search what I can't see," she said in a thin voice, then gulped.

"You search the parlor," Fabian said with a smile. "I'll check the shelves."

They spent a good hour going through both rooms with a fine-toothed comb, but once again, they came up with nothing. Fabian's stomach growled in protest at having skipped breakfast, and his nerves wore thin. They had to find something, anything, to prove Lord Stan-hope's guilt. He would marry Alice even against his mother's wishes if he had to and whisk her away to his Italian lands—as soon as he was certain they were still his —but he was loath to upset his mother or break with her in any way.

"We have to keep searching," he told Alice when she wilted with defeat. "Where else would your father think to hide something that no one would find and that he could retrieve later?"

Alice brushed a dusty hand along her disheveled hair. She had a smudge of dirt on her cheek and she was pink and sweaty with exhaustion, but she was still the most beautiful woman Fabian had ever known. Particularly when she flashed from disappointed to inspired, standing straighter, her eyes shining.

"The greenhouse," she said, her smile returning. "He was where he shouldn't have been in the greenhouse the day after we arrived."

Confidence filled Fabian once more. "The greenhouse it is, then."

But once again, after more than an hour of searching, all Fabian and Alice found were neglected pots, flowers that needed to be transplanted, and a family of mice that had taken up residence near one of the stoves that kept the greenhouse warm.

"He's going to win." Alice burst into tears as they met up near the display Fabian had made the day after her arrival. "My father is going to convince your mother that I'm a thief and a whore, and he'll take me away and marry me off to someone horrible."

"No," Fabian said, closing his arms around her and holding her close. "I won't allow it. I would never allow it."

"But how can you stop him?" Alice cried against his shoulder. "Your mother will hate me, and her husband is a duke. If a duke says I have to go, then I'll have to go."

"Then we'll go together." Fabian stroked her head, resting his cheek against her hair. "We'll go to Italy, even if we have to make our own way until my lands are sorted out. I promise you, Alice, I will never let your father come between us, and I will not let him go unpunished."

"But how can you stop him?" Alice sniffled. "He always wins, no matter how evil he is."

Fabian was ready to tell her he didn't know, but he would move heaven and earth to make things right, when a small sound near the greenhouse door caught his attention. He twisted with Alice still in his arms to find the maid who had been in her room earlier standing just inside the doorway, glancing this way and that, as though a demon would jump out and devour her at any moment. Instinctively, he knew the maid was the key to victory.

"You there, Beth, is it?" he called to her.

"Yes, my lord," the maid replied. She rushed away from the door and along the narrow aisles of plants to the center of the greenhouse.

"What is it?" Fabian asked on. He could see in her eyes she'd come to the greenhouse specifically to speak to them.

"I can't go on," poor Beth wailed, bursting into tears the same way Alice had. "I can't, I can't."

"It's all right," Fabian said, using every ounce of patience he had not to grab hold of the woman and shake whatever it was out of her.

"He's horrible," Beth continued to weep. "I didn't want to do any of it, but he said he'd have me fired and thrown out in the streets if I didn't do as he demanded. He said he'd make sure I had no choice but to become a dirty whore if I didn't help him."

A rush of triumph pushed through Fabian. Alice must have felt it as well. She stood straight and blinked away her tears.

"What did my father ask of you?" She stepped forward to put a comforting hand on the maid's arm.

"He gave me a sack full of valuable things and told me to hide it in your trunk, my lady," Beth squeaked through her tears. "He told me to make sure it would be found when you tried to leave."

"Where is that sack now?" Fabian demanded, trying not to frighten the poor girl with the force of his anger.

With shaking hands, Beth reached under her apron, untied something, and drew out a small sack. She handed it to Fabian as though it were poison, then burst into another sob, shaking from head to toe.

"He said he would blame it all on me if I told anyone," she wailed. "But I didn't steal anything, I didn't. You have to believe me."

"I believe you," Alice said instantly, wrapping her arm around Beth's back. "I know what kind of a man my father is."

The sack was heavy, and when Fabian opened it, all manner of gold and gems winked back at him. There were enough purloined goods in the small sack to sell for a fortune, the fortune Lord Stanhope needed.

"I believe you as well," he said, closing the sack and clenching his fist around the top. "We must take this to my mother at once."

"I'm so afraid," Beth continued to weep. "High sorts

blame low sorts, like me, all the time. What if the duchess believes Lord Stanhope? I don't want to be a whore. I'm a good girl."

"We won't let anything happen to you," Alice said. It amazed Fabian how quickly she had gone from being the one in distress to the one giving comfort with confidence. His heart swelled as he watched her hug Beth and smile at her reassuringly.

"Wicked men do more harm to themselves than good when backed against a wall," Fabian said, starting for the door and gesturing for the ladies to come with him. "I have no doubt that, given the chance, Lord Stanhope will incriminate himself when confronted."

They headed back through the frosty garden toward the house. Evening was already beginning to fall, and the servants that weren't still cleaning up from the ball rushed about, lighting lanterns and making the decorations adorning the house look every bit as festive as Christmas Eve demanded. The interior of the house was brimming with holly and mistletoe as well, and the delicious scent of supper wafted up from downstairs as they passed one of the servant's entrances.

"Find Lord Stanhope and bring him to my mother and the duke at once," Fabian ordered one of the footmen as they marched through the house.

The young man nodded and rushed off.

They found Fabian's mother, the duke, Matthew, and Georgette in a small, cozy family parlor toward the back of the house.

"Mama, I have the proof you need," Fabian announced as he strode into the room, Alice and Beth following. He held up the sack of loot, dropping it into his mother's lap when they reached the sofa where she sat.

"What is this?" his mother asked, somewhat uselessly, as she opened the sack. She answered her own question with a gasp.

"Beth, please explain," Fabian said, stepping to Alice's side and sliding a hand protectively around her waist while nodding to the maid.

"He forced me to help him, my lady," Beth began, shaking like an ice-covered bough in the wind, her voice barely above a whisper. "Lord Stanhope told me to hide it all in Lady Alice's trunk so that you would find it there."

"Good heavens." Fabian's mother pressed a hand to her chest as she handed the sack to the duke.

Beth continued with her story, but she had only just begun to explain Lord Stanhope's attempt at blackmail before the bastard himself strode into the room, two of Holly Manor's largest footmen flanking him like jailors.

"I have never been so insulted in all my life," he began before being addressed. "I will not let this attack stand. That little witch is lying. You should hear what she offered to do for me the other night."

Beth burst into fresh tears and rushed to the side of the room, as if she would hide behind one of the potted pine trees.

Lord Stanhope looked as though he would pursue her, but Matthew stepped into his path.

"How do you know what poor Beth has said?" Matthew demanded.

Lord Stanhope stopped, his mouth dropping open. It flapped for a moment before he said, "She's obviously a liar."

"What would she be lying about?" the duke asked, standing by Matthew's side.

"She—" Lord Stanhope gulped, glancing from the duke and Matthew to Beth to the duchess. His eyes finally came to rest on the sack of stolen goods, which the duke had put on a small table beside the sofa. "There!" he shouted triumphantly. "You found that in my daughter's trunk, no doubt. I bet she tried to escape without being noticed."

A bittersweet grin spread across Fabian's face and he turned to Alice as if to say he'd told her so.

"These items were not found in your daughter's possession," the duchess said, rising and stepping to her husband's side. "Beth brought them to my son. She explained how you attempted to blackmail her."

"See?" Lord Stanhope flung out his arm in Beth's direction. "I told you she was a liar."

"Yes, but you told us before any hint of a lie was brought forth," Fabian growled, eyes narrowed. "As if you already knew the story you were about to be told."

A hint of panic filled Lord Stanhope's eyes, as though he realized too late that he'd played his cards badly. "I...I only said she was a liar because all women are liars." Too late again, he glanced to Fabian's mother. "That is, all maids are liars."

"Beth has been a good and loyal servant these past five years," his mother said, a hardness accentuating the lines of her face in an expression Fabian knew all too well. His mother wasn't fooled. If Lord Stanhope was at all intelligent, he would run while he could.

But, of course, the man was a dolt. "Are you insinuating that I had something to do with this?" he bellowed, his acting as pitiful as his intentions. Not a soul in the room believed him, but he preened and sniffed as though he had been badly wronged. "I refuse to stand by and be treated this way. Come, Alice. We are leaving this place at once."

"My fiancée is going nowhere with you," Fabian said, glaring at the man. "And I advise, my lord, that you have all of Lord Stanhope's things thoroughly searched. He would not have offered all of his plunder for discovery unless he held back an even greater share to line his pockets later."

"Very wise," the duke said. He gestured to the footmen, who grabbed Lord Stanhope's arms and held them fast. "Search everything. And call the constable while you're at it."

"You cannot have me arrested," Lord Stanhope shouted. "I am an earl, a peer of the realm. The law does not apply to me."

"We shall see about that," the duke said. He gestured for the footmen to remove Lord Stanhope from the room.

"I may be needed for the search," he told the rest of them before following the footmen out.

"I'll help too," Matthew said, hurrying after him.

"And I'll see that Beth is settled," Georgette said, fetching Beth from the corner and leading her from the room.

"My dear, please forgive me for doubting your innocence for even a moment," Fabian's mother said, approaching Alice with a kind smile.

"I forgive you completely, my lady," Alice said, looking as though she'd rode through a thousand storms and come out intact but exhausted. "You had no reason to trust me, especially with my father speaking against me."

"I should never have believed such a villain," Fabian's mother went on. "I should have believed my son when he told me you are the perfect daughter-in-law. I'm certain we will come to know each other quite well now."

"Thank you, my lady."

Fabian's heart swelled in his chest as his mother embraced Alice as though she were her own. He could see a beautiful future ahead of them, all of them.

"If you do not mind, Mama," he said, gently taking Alice from her arms and folding her in his. "I believe my fiancée could use a meal and a rest. She should sleep well tonight, now that she has been let out of her captivity."

"Agreed," his mother said, her smile turning sympathetic. "You must rest well, my dear, for tomorrow is your wedding day."

CHAPTER 10

Christmas Day dawned bright and fresh, with a dusting of snow that made the world glitter as though it were covered with diamonds. Alice had never awoken so happy in her life. She was greeted by sunlight pouring through her window, a warm, cheery fire dancing in the grate, her wedding dress laid out over the end of the bed, and the sure and certain knowledge that her father would never harass her, or anyone else, ever again.

With the duke's help and influence, every bit of jewelry and coin that had been stolen the night of the ball and before was found. Better still, it was found among Alice's father's things, much of which had already been loaded into a carriage, as if he intended to make a speedy retreat. Her father was exposed as a thief and a liar and banished from Holly Manor. More than that, the duke vowed to use all of his influence to make certain that Alice's father would be shunned in good society, even though, as a nobleman, it would be difficult to bring legal charges against him.

Alice hadn't seen hide nor hair of her father before he left Holly Manor, fleeing to whatever dark fate awaited him, and she didn't care. She promised herself she'd write to her Uncle Richard at once, informing him of everything, and of the likelihood that he would inherit the Stanhope title and lands in due course. She thought about penning the letter as soon as she woke up, but excitement about her impending wedding made it impossible for her to sit for more than three minutes on end, let alone compose her thoughts enough to write such a delicate letter. She thought about writing to Imogen as well, to tell her it was safe to come out of whatever hiding she and Lord Thaddeus had gone into, and to Lettuce. Perhaps there was a way to free her sister from her miserable marriage and to bring her home from America after all.

"My, you do look lovely," Georgette said, interrupting Alice's scattered thoughts as she entered the bedroom. Alice hadn't even heard her knock.

"I feel like a feather tossed in the wind," she said with a laugh, sending a grateful smile to Beth, who had helped her dress and style her hair.

"I can imagine." Georgette crossed to her and closed her in a sisterly embrace. "I simply cannot believe that you have endured so much at the hands of your father. But all that is over now."

"Thank God," Alice sighed.

"And I am quite certain that Fabian will love and cherish you as no woman has ever been loved or cherished," Georgette went on.

"I pray the same will be true for you when you and Lord Loamley marry." Alice hugged her back.

Another maid arrived in the room with tea and cakes, but Alice could barely eat a bite. Time snuck up on her, and before she knew it, Georgette escorted her downstairs to where Fabian's mother was waiting. The three of them bundled up in fur cloaks and hurried across the grounds of Holly Manor to the family's chapel at the edge of the property.

Everything was perfect. The small chapel had been decorated as befitted the season, with boughs of the holly that gave the estate its name, ribbons, and candles. Alice felt as though she had stepped into a dream as she glanced around the magical space. That feeling blossomed further when Fabian and Matthew joined them.

"You are the most beautiful thing I've ever seen," Fabian whispered to her as he led her to the front of the chapel where the vicar waited. "I've never been prouder of anything than I am of marrying you."

Tears of joy stung at Alice's eyes. "And I am beyond happy to be marrying you," she said, blinking up at him. "You've saved me in so many ways."

"We've saved each other," he said.

For a moment, Alice was certain he would kiss her. But with the vicar and his family and most of the guests who were staying at Holly Manor for the party looking on, he restrained himself. Instead, he led Alice the rest of the way to the vicar, then stood by her side as the ceremony was carried out.

It all seemed to happen so fast. With a few, beautiful words, Alice and Fabian became man and wife. Alice could never have imagined that her heart would feel so light as she said the words binding her to Fabian forever. She'd thought she would be so miserable, that she was forced into the union, but the truth couldn't have been more different. Her father may have set up the match as a way to increase his own fortune, but the marriage, the love that flowered between her and Fabian, was theirs and theirs alone.

The wedding breakfast was far grander than anything Alice could have expected. It was more than just a celebration of two people becoming one, it was Christmas. The food was exceptional. Song and merriment reigned. The family opened its doors to distribute gifts of food and drink to the poor of the neighborhood, then another grand feast was held in the evening.

By the time Alice and Fabian retired to his bedroom for the night, Alice was so exhausted and full, and her head spun with the wine she'd consumed, that she didn't see how she could possibly live up to whatever plans Fabian had for their wedding night.

"You will simply have to ravish my slumbering body without my participation," she said with a sigh, sitting on the bed, then flopping to her back, arms outstretched, eyes closed. "I don't think I can move after the day this has been."

"Oh, I'll make you move, all right," Fabian said in a low purr.

When he didn't immediately join her on the bed, Alice opened one eye to peek at him. He'd taken a seat by the fire and was removing his boots. She giggled, remembering how difficult it had been to remove them the other night, a swirl of restless desire waking her up a bit. She pretended she was still too tired to move, but watched him all the same.

Fabian grinned at her, as if he knew she was coming alive but pretending not to, and tossed his boots aside. He stood, unbuttoning his jacket and waistcoat and tossing them carelessly aside as well. Heat infused Alice from head to toe, coalescing in her sex, as he tugged his shirt off over his head and went to work on the fastenings of his breeches. He made quick work of those as well, and within a minute, he was fully naked, clearly aroused, and stalking toward her.

Alice feigned a yawn and said, "Well, then, goodnight."

"Goodnight, my love," Fabian said, his voice suggesting anything but sleep.

He reached the edge of the bed and lifted her feet to remove her shoes, then slid his hands up her legs to loosen her garters and roll her thick stockings down. Alice shivered at the light brush of his hands against her calves, and even more when he traced lazy lines up her thighs, lifting the hem of her gown as he did. She resisted the urge to wriggle her legs wider and to give him easy access to the part of her that was now throbbing for him.

"I wonder what I can do to bring you pleasant dreams?" he went on, sensuality thick in his voice.

Alice answered by pretending to snore, but that clumsy sound turned into a gasp as he bunched her skirts around her waist, exposing her completely below the waist. It was all she could do not to throw her legs wide.

She was rewarded for her patience as he shifted closer to the bed, drawing circles on her knees, then hooking his fingers under them to tickle the sensitive skin there. It was surprisingly erotic, and Alice's breath hitched at his touch.

She lost the ability to breathe entirely as he pulled her knees wide apart in a sudden and commanding move. The whisper of cool air against her hot sex left her moaning in anticipation, but he continued to take his time, driving her wild with desire as he dragged his fingernails slowly up her inner thighs. She could feel her sex weeping for him as he came closer and closer to touching her there and mewled in protest when he stopped just short.

"Sleeping Beauty was awakened with a kiss, wasn't she?" he asked, a carnal rumble in his chest.

Alice sighed, "Perhaps."

Fabian laughed low in his throat as he knelt beside the bed. For a split second, Alice was confused by the action, until he planted a sensual kiss on the inside of her thigh. She hummed at the sensation, gripping the bedclothes as he kissed her other inner thigh, slightly higher. He continued kissing her, coming closer and closer to her core, and Alice was suddenly glad she'd sat on the edge of the bed instead of climbing under the covers.

He tugged her hips closer as his kisses reached the apex of her thighs. Her breath came in ragged gasps and she instinctively moved her legs farther apart. When he brushed his tongue across her wet slit, she gasped and sighed.

"I told you Sleeping Beauty could be awakened with a kiss," he purred, sliding his hands up to tease her inner folds.

Alice was beyond reply. He leaned toward her, teasing her with his tongue again before kissing and caressing her sex with his lips. It was the most shockingly sensual act she ever could have imagined, and it shot pleasure straight to her core. Her breath came in tight pants as he tasted her, his tongue stroking her. When he closed his mouth over her clitoris and gently sucked while circling her, she let out a wordless sound of pleasure that bordered on a sob.

Her body was primed and ready, and his ministrations were so expert, that she was throbbing with release in no time. Her orgasm hit hard and deep, even more so when he slipped two fingers inside of her to feel her body's contractions. It felt so good to squeeze him, to come apart with pleasure, but in the back of her mind, she knew she wanted more.

Fabian rocked back, rising to his feet and leaning over her, planting his hands on either side of her shoulders. "Are you awake now, my bride?"

"Deliciously," Alice answered with a smile.

"Then let's get you out of this silly gown so that I can feast on your tits before fucking you until you scream."

His words shouldn't have aroused her so, but they did. She wriggled in more ways than one as he flipped her onto her stomach so that he could tug the ties of her gown, then pull it over her head. He rolled her back to her back and unlaced her stays, his brow knit in concentration as he undressed her. She should have done more to help him, but all she could think about was the bliss of submitting to him and letting him have his way with her. *The Secrets of Love* was right. Patience and submission were a glorious path to pleasure.

But she could only submit so much. As soon as Fabian discarded her chemise and repositioned her in the middle of the bed, as he bent to kiss her, she circled her hands around his hips, then closed them around his stiff cock and tight balls. He sucked in a breath, evidently surprised, then let out a deep sigh of pleasure.

"These are mine now," Alice said with a grin, stroking him gently and rubbing her thumb over his tip.

"They are," Fabian growled. "Yours and yours alone."

"I promise I will treat them well," she went on,

mischief making her giggle. "And I'll give them a good home."

"I should say so," he said, shifting position and lifting her hips so that he could drive home.

She sucked in a breath at the sudden invasion, making a sound of approval and pleasure. She squeezed around him, impatient for him to thrust within her until he found his release. But he still wasn't in a hurry.

"I want to fill you with babies," he hummed, bending down to kiss her. He balanced on one hand while caressing her breast with the other. "I want children laughing and running all around us and getting into as much trouble as we get into."

"I want that too," she sighed, arching her hips to encourage him to get on with the act of making them. "I want a life with you."

"And you shall have it," he said.

He began to move, slow and sensual at first, thrusting as deep as he could and driving Alice wild. He even went so far as to hook his arm under one of her legs, lifting it and twisting her into an impossible position that greatly increased her pleasure. It was only when he began to move faster that she realized why the position felt so familiar.

"You read my book," she gasped, barely capable of words.

"And I intend to try out every pose it suggested," he growled, thrusting faster.

Alice didn't know whether to laugh or sigh or moan

with pleasure. The sound that came out of her was a combination of all three. Her body was alive with coiling tension, and every one of Fabian's powerful thrusts sent her closer and closer to the edge. The author of *The Secrets of Love* was a genius, as far as Alice was concerned, and as her body burst into a second, throbbing orgasm, she didn't know whether to cry out Fabian's name or to bless the author.

Fabian seemed equally impressed, and within seconds of the crashing wave of her orgasm, he tensed and cried out as he spilled his seed within her. The moment was one of such perfect bliss, the melding of two souls into one after hardship that she hadn't been certain she could endure. The heat of love filled her even as the liquid sensation of spent passion overtook her, and when Fabian collapsed beside her, his energy drained, she curled herself in his arms.

"I love you," she sighed, her arms and legs entwined with his. "I love you more than I ever thought possible."

"And I love you," he replied, panting and stroking the side of her face. "Beyond reason. I will never let anyone hurt you ever again."

Alice smiled, a deep sense of peace filling her. She surged into him, kissing him with everything she had. She believed his promise, and she knew they would be happy and safe together for the rest of their lives.

EPILOGUE

The warm, Italian sun beat down on the veranda where Alice lay stretched out on a chaise that overlooked the glorious beauty of Fabian's ancestral lands. The sunshine and balmy breezes of Tuscany were heaven after the stress and gloom of England. Alice smiled at the faded pages of *The Secrets of Love* that she held in one hand, rereading her favorite passage about how to tease a mate into submission by making them wait for release, rubbing her round belly with the other. The baby wasn't due for a few more months, but she felt as though it were already part of the family.

"You look like a princess, content with her kingdom," Fabian said, striding out onto the veranda. He held a packet of letters, and as he came to sit on the chaise at her feet, he handed one to her.

"I am content with my kingdom," she said, closing her book and attempting to lean toward him for a kiss.

Fabian spared her having to struggle by inching closer and kissing her. She sank back against her cushions with a happy sigh.

That happiness was dented somewhat when his expression turned suddenly serious.

"What is it?" she asked, glancing to the letter he'd handed her with alarm. It bore postage marks from some-place called St. Kitts.

Before she could ask about that, Fabian said, "I've had a letter from your Uncle Richard."

St. Kitts was forgotten. Alice blinked and shifted to sit straighter. "Why would Uncle Richard be writing to you?"

Fabian hesitated before saying, "He was uncertain how you would take the news of your father's death."

Twin sensations of shock and relief hit Alice. She let out a breath and sagged into her pillows. "Thank God."

Fabian's brow inched up. "You are not upset?"

Alice considered his question. "I am sad," she decided. "But more over the fact that he was such a horrible man, a man who wasted his life." She paused then asked, "How did he die?"

Fabian continued to look uncertain. "It is believed he took his own life after a night of drinking and gambling in which he lost more than he was worth."

Heaviness descended on Alice's shoulders and she lowered her head. "I wish I could say I was surprised."

"But you're not," Fabian said. It wasn't a question. He shifted closer to her, cleared his throat, and nodded to the letter in her hands. "That one baffles me. Who would be writing to you from the Caribbean?"

Alice blinked and glanced from the letter to Fabian and back again. "Is that where St. Kitts is?"

"Yes." Fabian's smile returned. "Open it."

Alice instantly tore into the letter. "It must be from Lettuce," she said. "She's the only person I know outside of Europe and—" She gasped as she recognized her sister's handwriting. "It is from Lettuce."

"Go on," Fabian said with a grin, prompting her.

Alice scanned the first few lines, then read. "*Dearest Alice. I was surprised and delighted to hear from Imogen that you have left England for Italy. I'd sent a letter to you at home, but I'm sure you haven't received it. So I shall have to write my entire story over again.*"

"Story?" Fabian asked. "What story?"

Alice glanced up at him, then continued. "*I have been through an adventure like nothing you could ever imagine in the last year, like something out of a fairy story. It began with a miserable marriage to a vain and abusive groom of father's choosing and took a turn for the worse as my horrible husband dragged me onto a ship bound for America. But everything changed when the pirates attacked....*"

❧

139

I hope you have enjoyed Alice and Fabian's story! But I just know you're dying to hear what happened to Lettuce. Well, Lettuce's story, *The Captured Vixen*, will be available as part of the Once Upon a Pirate box set, available now!

And if you would like to read about Imogen and Thaddeus, be sure to look for *The Faithful Siren*.

If you're interested in reading about the wild, summer house party thrown by the Herringtons, the party where Alice and Fabian met, be sure to look for the House Party trilogy of the *When the Wallflowers were Wicked* series: *The Devilish Trollop*, *The Playful Wanton*, and *The Charming Jezebel*, all available now!

If you enjoyed this book and would like to hear more from me, please sign up for my newsletter! When you sign up, you'll get a free, full-length novella, *A Passionate Deception*. Victorian identity theft has never been so exciting in this story of hope, tricks, and starting over. Part of my *West Meets East* series, *A Passionate Deception* can be read as a stand-alone. Pick up your free copy today by signing up to receive my newsletter (which I only send out when I have a new release)!

Sign up here: http://eepurl.com/cbaVMH

Click here for a complete list of other works by Merry Farmer.

ABOUT THE AUTHOR

I hope you have enjoyed *The Holiday Hussy*. If you'd like to be the first to learn about when new books in the series come out and more, please sign up for my newsletter here: http://eepurl.com/cbaVMH And remember, Read it, Review it, Share it! For a complete list of works by Merry Farmer with links, please visit http://wp.me/P5ttjb-14F.

Merry Farmer is an award-winning novelist who lives in suburban Philadelphia with her cats, Torpedo, her grumpy old man, and Justine, her hyperactive new baby. She has been writing since she was ten years old and realized one day that she didn't have to wait for the teacher to assign a creative writing project to write something. It was the best day of her life. She then went on to earn not one but two degrees in History so that she would always have something to write about. Her books have reached the Top 100 at Amazon, iBooks, and Barnes & Noble, and have been named finalists in the prestigious RONE and Rom Com Reader's Crown awards.

ACKNOWLEDGMENTS

I owe a huge debt of gratitude to my awesome beta-readers, Caroline Lee and Jolene Stewart, for their suggestions and advice. And double thanks to Julie Tague, for being a truly excellent editor and assistant! Thanks also to the members of the Historical Harlots Facebook Group, who provide me with all sorts of inspiration!

Click here for a complete list of other works by Merry Farmer.

Printed in Great Britain
by Amazon